The Poet and The Echo is a stunning collection of poems from the past paired with new short stories. Each thought-provoking tale responds to the original text in ways that send a reverberation back in time, which not only changes our understanding of what came before but also enriches our sense of the present. The result is like two palms pressed together across the ages – the space inbetween becoming a place to listen carefully for hidden truths. A wonderful collection to experience and enjoy.

– Sophie Haydock, author of *The Flames*

THE POET AND THE ECHO

Based on the BBC series
The Poet and the Echo,
first broadcast on BBC Radio 4

First published in 2023
by Scratch Books Ltd.
London

Introductory material © Kirsty Williams, 2023

Jacket design © Claire Goble, 2023
Typesetting by Will Dady, 2023

The moral rights of the contributing authors
of this anthology to be identified as such is
asserted in accordance with the Copyright,
Designs and Patents Act of 1988.

"BBC" and "Radio 4" are registered
trademarks of the British Broadcasting
Corporation and are used under licence.

All rights reserved. No part of this publication may be
reproduced, stored in a retrieval system, or transmitted in any
form or by any means, electronic, mechanical photocopying,
recording, or otherwise, without the prior permission of both
the copyright owner and the above publisher of this book.

This is an anthology of fiction. All characters, organisations,
and events portrayed in each story are either products
of each author's imagination
or are used fictitiously.

Printed in Gloucester by Severn

ISBN Paperback 9781739830144

Contents

Introduction Kirsty Williams	VII
To Enter the Garden Leila Aboulela	3
The Lamb Pippa Goldschmidt	15
Musical Speeches David Almond	25
Philomel @ Nightingale Jenni Fagan	37
The Idler Hannah Lavery	47
The Garden Jessie Greengrass	57
He Wishes for the Cloths of Heaven PK Lynch	69
Carpe Diem Cathy Forde	79
The Grey Eagle Harry Josephine Giles	91
On Being Brought from Africa to America Fred D'Aguiar	103

Introduction

by Kirsty Williams

As makers of audio programmes, we are always looking for hooks in time, works that make connections and show old ideas in new ways. For a long while, we wanted to bring some poetry into our output, but we are the Audio Drama and Readings team at BBC Scotland; our focus is on 'stories' and 'drama'; 'poetry' is not our remit.

That was until 2015 when, searching a database of anniversaries, we found the hook that would allow us to marry poetry and prose: the 150th birthday of W.B. Yeats. Taking inspiration from his anniversary and his 1938 poem, 'The Man and the Echo' – a contemplation of life, death, art and humanity written just before he died – we suggested to BBC Radio 4 a series of short stories inspired by his work. *Yeats: The Man and the Echo* would broadcast a poem (by Yeats) and a story written in response to it ('the echo') in juxtaposition, for listeners to enjoy together.

We found that the series gave writers an opportunity to delve into something both lyrical and affecting, to tell stories infused with the potency of another writer's vision. Their works formed moving meditations on the contemporary world, capturing the inner lives of characters who've stepped out of words carved in a different century.

The stories were so unusual and illuminating that the following year we went back to Radio 4 and offered them a recurring series – a broader interpretation of the idea, to include poets from all eras and all nationalities. Radio 4 agreed to commission it and so *The Poet and the Echo* was born.

In the years since, we've commissioned 28 stories for the series. Whilst working mostly with Scottish writers, we also commission artists from across the UK. Some, like David Almond and Jenni Fagan, are celebrated novelists. Other contributors, such as Leila Aboulela and Jessica Greengrass, are award-winning short story writers. We also commissioned artists whose voices have been honed for the spoken word, like Hannah Lavery, whose work is predominantly in poetry and performance, and P.K. Lynch, a playwright and actor as well as a novelist. The choice is deliberately eclectic – like any good story collection, we want to inspire with the richness and diversity of these arrayed pieces.

Once we have approached a writer, we ask them to find an out-of-copyright poem they would like to respond to, drawing inspiration in whatever way they wish, to create a new short story.

Where some of the poets are not widely known, the stories act as introductions, such as to vital works like that of the mixed-heritage poet and activist, Alice Moore Dunbar-Nelson, born in America a decade after the Civil War, or Anne Finch, an English poet and part of the Royal Court during the turbulent years of the late 17th and early 18th century.

When our contemporary writers reach back to such poets, they amplify the value of their original words, bringing them to the attention of a broader audience to give us new ways to understand ourselves and others.

And the stories these writers create are more than simple echoes; by looking back into an older work, they create a unique weaving together of artistic expression that becomes the key to a new fictional world, opening up intriguing paths to reappraise the context and meaning of the poems they sprung from. Our poets offer up a thread of feeling that – like Yeats' imagery of the stars in 'He Wishes for the Cloths of Heaven' – spans across our vision to create endless patterns, joyous re-imaginings, and powerful portraits of the human condition.

Kirsty Williams – producer and director at BBC Scotland.

THE POET AND THE ECHO

To Enter the Garden

Leila Aboulela

Happy when we sat in the palace, you and I
With two bodies but one soul, you and I
The colours of the grove and the sounds of the birds will be forever
When the time comes to enter the garden, you and I
The stars will come to gaze upon us
And we will show them the moon, you and I
You and I, separate now, will join in ecstasy
Joyful and safe from useless chatter, you and I

'The Union of Minds'
From the *Diwan-e Shams-e Tabrizi* by Jalalul-Din Rumi

Deep in Christendom they left him, until his half-brother's claim to the throne was suppressed. It was a plan formulated as his father lay dying. Selim was still too young – in the struggle for succession that exploded even before the sultan's soul departed, his heir was vulnerable. Selim's every meal was first tasted by the harem's eunuch, every time he wanted to step out onto the balcony a surveillance of possible sharp-shooters was necessary. He would be safer far away in the hills of North Italy. Only a trusted few knew that he was in the palace high above Lake Como, a prince without a retinue, a youth without daily guidance, a guest of sorts. All he had to do was wait. It would not be long, they reassured him.

The palace was built above terraced gardens. Summer shimmered over the lake. The water was still, cupped between the mountains. There was not a single breeze, nor the song of birds, nor the shriek of forest animals.

Slung between the mountain slopes, tucked out of sight, this was the perfect getaway, behind tall locked gates, up miles of stairs, one layered garden after the other, olive trees with their silver leaves, pomegranates sagging on the branches; small smelly yellow fruit he could not name. He explored the grounds, studied a fresco he came upon, a coat of arms. High above was the ruins of a castle, an eyrie but he was on top of the world. He ran down all the way to the lake. He watched the gardeners sprinkle the grass and tend the trees. He had more freedom than he had ever had in his normal life, if the life of a future sultan could ever be normal. A prince too old for the harem but still too young for the brutal world of men. An awkward age. His voice, new to him and unreliable, was not needed in the villa. Apart from the servants, the palace was deserted, the family who lived in it were away for the summer. Selim could not speak Italian to the servants. They cleaned his room, washed his clothes and served him his meals. Someone must have informed them about the pork.

One day there was a visit from the ambassador to Italy, Ekrem Pasha. He did not come empty-handed. He brought Selim extra clothes, a carpet, two boxes of Turkish Delight and a concubine. The girl was dark-skinned and taller than Selim. Her lips stretched over her teeth as if she was suppressing a laugh. Her eyes sparkled and looked straight at him. He noted the colour of her head wrap, the matching string of beads round her neck. "The girl will keep you company," Ekrem Pasha said. As usual he spoke slowly, his heavy-lidded eyes giving little away, his voice low and elegant. "She can sing, dance and tell stories. We must not allow your Majesty to get lonely."

Selim was only lonely during meal-times, not when he was outdoors. In the gardens, he was never alone. The olive trees, the almost ripe pomegranates, the lizards and the vines – they were enough. But he chose not to contradict the ambassador. The girl's name was Fatou. She spoke his language. In fact, she spoke several languages, including Italian. When Ekrem Pasha left, Selim showed her around the palace and the grounds. Despite her confidence, she was bewildered by her surroundings, confused by the circular paths, the steps that served as a short-cut to the palace. Selim ran towards the lake and she followed. Like he did every afternoon, he took off his shirt and waded into the water.

"I don't know how to swim," she said and sat on the shore. She played with the pebbles on the sand instead of watching him. When he came out of the water, he saw that she had dug several holes and divided the pebbles into two equal portions. As the sun dried his skin, she taught him a new game. The pebbles were seeds, she explained, and to win he must sow the greatest number of seeds.

Looking down at the pebbles and the sand, they were both absorbed. He frowned when things didn't go his way. She rubbed sand between her fingers when she was considering a move. He played in order to win while she took pleasure in the strategies. He sat up straight as he had been taught, cross-legged and upright. She stretched her legs out, stuffed the folds of her skirt between them and hunched her back. "Don't rush," she said to him. "Take your time. Tease your opponent before you win." He started to feel thirsty.

When they climbed back up to the palace, the lizards made her squeal. Every time they each put a foot down, a lizard would dart out of the way. Right foot, left foot, her right, his right, her left, his left. It sounded like a chant, right foot, left foot. The way she said it, her voice melodious and rich. "Oh look at that fat one!" she laughed out. He knew she wanted to catch one, to hold it in her palm and squeeze its stomach. It made him laugh. And when he laughed, she laughed too.

Fatou did not sit with him while he ate. She took her food and sat on the floor, eating with her fingers. She positioned herself in such a way that he didn't need to crane his neck to look at her. He sat at the dining table with a tablecloth and a napkin, the European way. He wanted to ask her to sit with him. If he did, it would be an order she would have to obey. He would have preferred to sit with her. Back home, there would be a low table with a cushioned stool, the meal coming in large round trays, the food tastier.

When Fatou finished eating, and before the dessert was served, she stretched out on her side, away from him, and slept. He ate grapes and watched her sleeping. She had used her arm as a pillow. She was tired from her journey, even though she had only travelled from the ambassador's home in Sardinia. Selim's journey had been longer, and he too had arrived fatigued and sleepy, a little seasick even, shocked not by his father's death, but by the separation from all he had known. The danger he did not feel, but everyone else had stressed it so it must be real. He did not know his half-brother well, though in age they were only a few months apart. They had different mothers, rivals who hated each other. He remembered a day out hunting with his father and siblings. He remembered them lining up to kiss the Sultan's hand, Selim ahead of the others because he was the oldest. He remembered the Sultan murmuring, you are brothers, united, stay loyal to each other. But the mothers, from different sects, taught the children otherwise. And now this was the destiny that the mothers had set.

When Selim finished eating, he strolled over and looked down at her. To fall asleep while her king was awake, lazy girl. He should kick her awake. She would jump up startled and apologise. Instead he poked her hips with his toe, felt the digging into soft flesh, resisted the impulse to pinch and twist. She shifted and sighed but didn't wake up. He left her and walked out into the garden.

The heat gripped the gardens and the villas. Lethargic, he sat on the only stone bench that was in the shade and closed his eyes. Strange that there were no sounds of birds. At home there would have been parakeets and redwings, curlews and kingfishers. He heard the crunch of gravel and knew it was her. Without opening his eyes, he saw the space around him change from aloneness to togetherness, from isolation to company. "We do not want you to get lonely," Ekrem Pasha had said. But he had not known that he was lonely. He had been too busy tasting freedom. The lack of routine, the absence of duty, for the first time aimless, for the first time ignored, stripped of importance. And now she was here for a purpose. Selim knew what a concubine was for. What role she played. But that was the adult world not his. Just like ruling an empire, ascending the throne, leading an army. Things that were going to happen when he grew up. One day. Not now, not soon. And yet the future had arrived. His childhood was coming to an end.

"You're ready?" He heard her contradict his thoughts. She was older than him, perhaps by a year or two, and though less educated, she was more mature, more knowledgeable. She had grown up in slavery, never known who her parents were, never known who had carried her across desert and sea to sell her in the markets of Istanbul. The only clue she had was her skin. The only factual part of the story. The rest were unreliable memories, sand dunes and a woman's voice singing her to sleep, the laughter of her people.

"You are from Africa," he said to her. And told her everything he had been taught about the continent. "Have you not met others like yourself?"

"Slaves yes, but not from Africa." There was an edge in her voice when she said the word 'slaves'; wonder when she said the word she had just learned – 'Africa'. They were walking again, down to the lake. The sun was softer and there was more shade.

The lizards again. Darting between their feet. She chanted again – right foot, left foot, but more slowly than she had done before. He picked up the melody and it stayed with him.

How many days did they spend together? How many weeks? Until the season turned. Gusts of wild winds blowing her skirt, making them shriek and cling to each other. Making them hold on to the walls as if they were in danger of being lifted and tossed into the lake. The first nip of autumn. The pomegranates on the trees, heavier and riper, dragging the branches to the ground. Days spent wandering the palace, gazing at the paintings – her favourite the one of the washer-woman, his the snow-capped mountains. Nights that were too cold to spend gazing up at the stars. Nights in which the fires of the palace were lit.

How many days did they spend together? How many meals and times did she sing her right foot, left foot chant which he started singing too until it stayed in his mind. It stayed longer than anything else. All the memories faded except for the right foot, left foot, right, left, which would float up on him as he climbed stairs, without her.

It all ended abruptly. The day they quarrelled was the same day his exile ended. Bitterness sealed the beauty and obstructed any nostalgia. On that last day there was no time to make amends, no time to clear the misunderstanding, no time to say: sorry, I had no right to be cruel.

It started when she said, "we will be here until they kill your brother. In your name, they will kill him."

"Of course not," he said but he did not push her away, not yet. He did not untangle himself from her embrace, lift his arm, roll away.

She laughed out loud. "But what else do you expect? Don't you understand why you are out of the way? Not only so that you won't be killed but so that *he* would be the one killed."

It made him furious that she would dare speak like that. "What do you know?" He humiliated her. He used words that brought pain to her eyes. They drew apart. One hour, two hours and he would have started to miss her, to search for her, to win her back with sweet words and caresses. But it was as if the world surged up and clattered into their paradise. The ambassador arrived, and he was not alone this time. A whole battalion came with him. Men on horses. Men with flags. A carriage, trunks full of robes and turbans for the new sultan.

"You have triumphed over your enemies," the ambassador said. And Selim knew better than to ask about the fate of his half-brother.

He never saw Fatou again. They left the palace and went separate ways. She went back to her mistress, the ambassador's wife. Months later, accompanying her on the pilgrimage in Mecca, Fatou saw her people for the first time. People who looked like her, laughed in the same way, their voices her voice. She could not leave them after she had found them. In the throngs surrounding the Holy Ka'ba, it was not difficult to slip away, to join the African pilgrims in their journey home. They sailed over the Red Sea and tracked their way through the deserts of Sudan. They headed west until they reached their home in Mauritania. Fatou was in the Africa of her dreams, the Africa Selim had told her about.

Selim, the sultan, wearing the legendary sword and decorated belt, grew into his titles – Emperor of the East, Allah's deputy on Earth, King of the Believers and Unbelievers. He had shed his childhood in North Italy. He had given his innocence to Fatou.

They forgot each other. How could they not when all the true adventures happened after they separated? Fatou's escape from slavery and her epic journey westwards across Africa. Selim ruling an empire, leading armies, forging treaties, fighting enemies. Fatou immersed herself in learning the language and customs of her people. The songs, the dances, the clothes. She would never be lonely again. A man, very poor but a good husband and then one child after the other. She became a fierce mother and with every fresh love she bestowed on a new-born, the memory of Selim faded away. She buried three children, not only a baby but a lovely ten-year old; her eldest went to seek his fortune and never came back. These losses, this pain wove itself through her. Sometimes, exhausted and asleep, she would dream of pomegranates ready to be eaten, she would feel her body light and healthy again, her tongue sharp, the gurgle of heavenly laughter in her throat.

If Selim could see her now, he would not recognize her. Not the woman with the sagging breasts, the scratch of white hair poking beneath her head-wrap. And she would not recognize him either. His manicured hands stained with justice, the turban thrust over the corpulent face, the wet lips that rarely smiled. So many women passed through his life. Wives and concubines. His tastes were noted, and slave girls were brought to him from Abyssinia and Zanzibar. But he did not remember Fatou's name even when a wife asked flirtishly, "who was the first woman that you bedded?" He did not remember Fatou's face even when there were mentions of Italy or the one-time ambassador there, Ekrem Pasha. What Selim remembered was the terraced gardens which with time became a kind of longing. Sometimes, too, climbing stairs in the open air, a melody would float in his head. Right foot, left foot, right, right. Left, left. He would hear her laughter again. And his laughter too. No, they were not destined to meet again. At least not in this life.

The Lamb

Pippa Goldschmidt

Little Lamb who made thee
　　Dost thou know who made thee

　　　　　　　　　From 'The Lamb' by William Blake

I'm in the kitchen with Mum who's heating up the beans. Mum cooks everything in the microwave, imprisons food behind the glass door so she can keep an eye on it, the digital display counting down the minutes. Just like her work at the agricultural institute, where everything living is converted into numbers; the sheep on the hill outside her office, how much they weigh, how many lambs they have, how good they are at feeding their lambs. All these births and lives and deaths are entered into her database and transformed into figures.

Now, while the beans are circling the inside of the microwave, she puts me in charge of buttering toast and makes me recite her directions, listening as I pick my way along the closely-packed words, 'Up Ridley Street and second turning on the left which is Dundonald Street. Walk down here until you get to the narrow alley and then cut through it, taking care to not step in all the rubbish, and come out onto Glenisle Road. Turn right and continue to the end to the kids' playground. Cross at a diagonal, avoiding the men sitting on the bench. Find the path at the other side that leads to the estate.'

'That leads to the estate,' repeats my mother. 'For the life of me I don't understand how you can parrot all this and then get lost every time you actually go there.'

There means my sister's flat where I'm sent every weekend, where I raise my head for her to trim my fringe and hear all about her hairdressing job – if I don't sit still, she says, I'll lose my eyelashes. A lot of the women who come into the hairdressers ask for her by name, she's that good apparently.

Mum never comes with me to my sister's. When I ask why, she's never said. I've spent my life watching sheep and how lambing ewes hide away at the highest points of the hill until the lamb's been born. But Mum has *always* stayed away by herself, away from Sis.

The next weekend I get lost again. I'm walking down a narrow street lined on either side with houses, fastened together as close as a zip. But I'm sure this is not where I'm supposed to be and it's only when I find the hill on the edge of the town that I can breathe again. If Mum had a mind to glance out of her bedroom window, she might see me in the distance, making my way up the twists and turns of the hill's sheep tracks, and wonder why I preferred it up here to down there. Then again, she probably wouldn't wonder. Mum has little time and even less inclination for wondering; the hill doesn't have a name and therefore it can't be part of her world.

But I feel more confident trusting the sheep tracks than Mum's instructions. Up here I can feel the wind lift all her words clean away from me.

By the time I'm perched on the bathtub, Sis examining her scissors above me, it's mid-afternoon. 'Only half an hour late today,' I say, 'that's better than usual, isn't it?'

'Where on earth do you get to?' she mutters, and she tousles my hair.

I shrug. I look down at my fingers, all covered with the pollen that drifts over the hill this time of year. In the air, it's invisible, free to go wherever it likes – it's strange, you can only see the pollen after it's already settled on you.

When Sis has finished sorting out my fringe, we sprawl on the sofa with the curtains pulled against the daylight. I like living in the dim afternoons of her flat, watching films and eating crisps. Sometimes when we squabble, Sis seems more my own age, even though she's fifteen years older than me. I can't remember the time when she lived at home with me and Mum.

At Mum's work, each sheep has its own number fastened to it by an ear tag. This number is linked to all sorts of information about the sheep's breeding history, not just its parents, but all the other sheep that it's related to. We can know a lot more about sheep families than our own, Mum tells me. Collecting these numbers helps to improve the sheep, she says, make them better at what they do.

They seem alright to me, I think.

Mum is also keen for me to do well, to pass tests. My reading age is above average – this is a good thing according to her. My maths abilities are below average and this makes her cross. Soon it will be the time for me to make choices at school, she says. What do I want to do with my life?

What do I want? To run my hands against more stalks of grass than I could ever count, to watch a nameless bird beat its wings high above me. To feel heat on my closed eyes and know the sun is shining on me.

Mum tells me not to be so silly.

At school, there's a picture of Jesus hanging in the main assembly hall, surrounded by a flock of sheep with a lamb tucked under one arm. Though real shepherds don't look anything like this; they zip around the hill on quad bikes, their dogs flopping across the back and grinning at me.

The sheep on the hill tend to keep their distance, particularly in the spring when they're lambing. If the ewes get separated from their lambs, they call for each other until they're reunited. It's not recognition by sight but something deeper than what eyes can see. When the lambs are old enough, the ewes show them where to find the sweetest grass and the most sheltered areas.

On the hill I quite often come across some old bones. A jaw-bone, with teeth still attached, or the flat fan of a shoulder bone. The sheep don't seem to care that they're surrounded by the bodies of their mothers or grandmothers. They just carry on nibbling. The sheep live on the hill, take their food from it and then, when their lives are over, they return to it.

One Saturday evening, Sis is showing me how to colour my hair. My fringe is turning bright blue, like the figures they spray on the sheep. 'You don't have to call me that, you know,' she says.

'Call you what?' I'm trying to look at my reflection in the mirror, but it's too high up and I can only see the top of my head.

She sighs, and sets the bottle of dye on the side of the sink and I realise I'm not totally sure what her real name is. 'Mary,' she says as if she can read my mind.

'Is that what they call you at the hairdressers?'

'Well, they wouldn't call me Sis, would they?'

'So why do *I* call you that?'

She stands up, and now she looks really cross for some reason, 'We're done here. I'll clean up and you choose the DVD.'

'Ok, Mary,' but it sounds odd to me.

The next evening, when I'm back home, I try it again, 'Mary cooked me a pizza for dinner last night.'

Mum pauses, a plate in each hand. She looks at me, but she doesn't speak.

I think, Did you teach me to call Sis Sis? The microwave pings and the door springs open, but it reveals nothing more interesting than warmed-up lasagne.

Then I think, Why do I call you Mum?

Mum tells me that her job is good because it's very secure. This makes me think of the high chain-metal fences around the agricultural institute, but apparently this is not what she means. She left school with nothing, she always says, and got pregnant when she was still very young. Then she started evening classes, and after that she did a degree at the OU. 'Look where I am now,' she says, 'and that's why you need to work harder, especially at maths.'

I tell Sis about this next weekend.

'She used to say that to me,' Sis says, 'She was banging on about it so much that I couldn't face it. I wanted to work with my hands. Work that isn't about flaming numbers and databases, that involves actual people. Mum can't stand the idea of it.'

'Is that why she's angry with you?'

'That and other things. Ancient history, kiddo.' She's packing her equipment away in her hairdresser's roll, the lines of scissors as neat as any medical instruments I've seen at the doctor's. 'Ancient history,' she repeats but her hands slip and the scissors spill out onto the lino, glinting in the fluorescent light.

'Mary?'

'Do what you want, kiddo.' She's kneeling on the floor, and I could just reach out and touch the top of her head, 'Do what you want with your life and don't listen to her.'

A few weeks later, on an evening when Mum is supervising my maths homework, the doorbell rings. It's Sis, but she hardly ever comes here. Maybe on Christmas day after lunch has been cleared away, maybe then. But not like this, not without Mum knowing in advance.

In the hallway, Sis is draping her coat on the bannister like I do every day when I get home from school. Only then do I understand properly that she used to live here when she was my age – just like I live here now. She walks down the hallway and opens the door into the living room, and I follow her, until she bangs the door shut and I'm left outside trying to hear what's going on.

'Just why do you want her to follow in your footsteps so badly?' this is Sis.

'Well, who would want her to follow in *yours*?' The same thing I've heard every day. But Sis has done fine. She enjoys her work, she likes making the ladies in the salon feel good about themselves. 'And what do you think you're doing, telling her to call you Mary?' Mum continues.

'It's my name!'

'It's not what we agreed.'

I don't want to listen anymore. I back away from the living room door and I leave the house.

No need to follow Mum's instructions now.

It's not until I'm nearly at the top of the hill that I turn around and look back down and I see two figures making their way up behind me. It's Mum and Mary. They're scrambling up the same sheep track that I used but it's too narrow for them to walk side by side, Mum's behind Mary and she keeps slipping on the loose stones, and she's falling behind – even from here I can see that Mary isn't slowing down to help Mum get her balance but keeping a steady pace towards me. Their voices rise up the hill, calling to me, shouting at me to stop, their voices echoing all around the hill and mingling with the rising call of the sheep.

There's a ewe in front of me, leading her lamb to a sheltered spot and I start to follow her. The light's dimmer now but I'm still able to see her white fleece, so I keep walking right over the top and out of sight, and I know that Mum and Mary will follow me wherever I go, wherever that happens to be.

Musical Speeches

David Almond

Birds all the summer day
Flutter and quarrel
Here in the arbour-like
Tent of the laurel.

Here in the fork
The brown nest is seated;
For little blue eggs
The mother keeps heated.

While we stand watching her
Staring like gabies,
Safe in each egg are the
Bird's little babies.

Soon the frail eggs they shall
Chip, and upspringing
Make all the April woods
Merry with singing.

Younger than we are,
O children, and frailer,
Soon in the blue air they'll be,
Singer and sailor.

We, so much older,
Taller and stronger,
We shall look down on the
Birdies no longer.

They shall go flying
With musical speeches
High overhead in the
Tops of the beeches.

In spite of our wisdom
And sensible talking,
We on our feet must go
Plodding and walking.

'Nest Eggs' by Robert Louis Stevenson

"Please, sir," said Sally Smith. "Robin Greed's a bird again, sir. Yes it's lovely, but he's putting me off my poem, sir."

I moved across the classroom to their table. Bent down to poor pale Robin. Smelt the unwashed sweat on him. Before him were the gifts the children gathered: feathers and abandoned nests, opened egg shells.

"Which song is it today," I whispered. "The blackbird? The thrush?"

Of course he couldn't say. He sang softly, sweetly. The sounds came from his lips, his tongue, his throat. To me it seemed they rose unfettered from his soul.

"And what is your poem, Sally?" I asked.

She flinched, surprised I'd even asked. She glared and pointed through the classroom window, past the chain-link fence, across the road, to the bulldozers and diggers that were gathered there.

LONG LIVE THE WILDERNESS was her title.

"What else is there to write about?" she said.
"Perhaps nothing," I said.
"Sing more softly, please," I said to Robin.
I tried to sing along with him.
Sally smiled, pencil poised before her in mid-air.
"What is it?" I said.
"Just thought how Robin looks like you, sir."
"Does he?"
I leaned closer to him, shared a moment of harmony.

Death had drawn me back. I was travelling in the east when I heard from Mum that Dad had died. By the time I got home, she'd followed him into the dark. I spent a year of grief and writing, yearning to hear them again, then chose to be a teacher. I took up my first appointment in the school I'd gone to myself, Moorgate, at the far edge of the great estate that filled this city's western slopes. I'd grown up in these streets. I used to play beyond the fence, in the wilderness where coal mines used to be, until my mother's voice sang out over the rooftops at dusk to call me home.

Now, the hedges and copses would be ripped away, the ponds would be drained, and another great estate, of executive homes, would appear out there.

I wanted the children to thrive and to change the world through art, through story and poetry, through drama and song. Their paintings hung on the walls with the work of Van Gogh, Picasso, Frida Kahlo. All that spring, we sang and chanted poems about growth, about flowers, about birds. We sang the unstoppable song of life.

One Monday morning, we marched across the road and stood at the fence with our placards and the children chanted Stevenson as if declaring war.

"Here in the fork
The brown nest is seated!
Four little blue eggs
The mother keeps heated!
While we stand watching her
Staring like gabies,
Safe in each egg are the
Bird's little BABIES!
Bird's little BABIES!
Bird's little BABIES!"

My friends in the media turned up as they said they would. The plucky protest was shown on *Look North*. Robin was with us, pale-faced and fragile, slumped on his crutches. The developers were shamed into delay. They'd wait till all eggs were hatched, all fledglings had flown.

The Head Teacher took me to his office. How was the children's progress? he asked. I said that the children were learning the power of poetry, community, protest. They were learning about politics, about the natural world. Was that enough? he asked. In a few weeks time the OFSTED Inspectors would be with us. Were the children prepared? At the time of my appointment the school was in Special Measures. The Head said I was one of a new generation who'd make such schools Outstanding.

"Are you still committed to that cause?" he asked.

I said that yes I was, and backed away.

"Robin Greed," he muttered.

"Robin Greed?"

"Perhaps we should arrange," he said, "to have him in the hospital when OFTSED is around."

I stared back at him.

"We don't want anything," he said, "that might hold the other children back."

"Hold them back?"

"We want them to thrive, don't we, just as you yourself have thrived?"

Had I thrived? Perhaps I had begun to. In the evenings I cycled to my apartment in the city and wrote there. My stories appeared in little magazines. A couple were broadcast on Radio 4. But poetry was my yearning. I wished to become Orphic, to exchange my throat for the throat of a bird and to let the songs flow through me as they seemed to flow through Robin Greed. How strange to find him in this place, my troubled little muse, as if he were some long-lost fragment of myself. I made recordings of him on my phone, played them as I wrote, tried to work the weird rhythms into my lines. No one would publish them, but in the scheme of things, that was nothing. I'd be writing for a lifetime, but Robin's songs would soon come to an end. Unlike his classmates, I knew how ill he was. The days when he wasn't with us, in the hospital school at the RVI, he wasn't only receiving physiotherapy and speech therapy but also the medicines that might keep at bay the disease that would kill him.

His mother, Kath, had been in my class at this school, had gone to the same secondary school, Balmoral Grange. A drinker with tattoos on her arms from the age of thirteen. A lass to keep away from, but a lass to whom many of us were drawn. My pal Kevin Duffy went out with her for a while in year 11. I was haunted by the thought that I'd spent a night with her myself during some drunken party back when I was seventeen.

She showed up at my first parents' evening. The blurry tattoos, the smell of cigarette smoke, the grainy voice.

She laughed.

"Kai," she said, using my old nickname with affection. "What the hell you doing back here, Kai?"

I shrugged the question away and we talked about her boy. She said his books didn't really matter, did they? His progress didn't really matter, did it? Right from the start, she knew how his life would be. He'd never thrived, never learned to speak. Mewed like a cat as a babe, barked like a dog as a bairn. Then the birds got into him and he'd stuck with that.

"And one day soon he'll fly away," she said.

"He seems… happy."

"Is he, Kai? How can *you* tell that?"

Her eyes grew cold, but she relaxed again. The pretty mischief still shone within her eyes.

"Come and see us," she said. "We'll share a glass or two."

I wondered: what if I'd stayed with a lass like Kath and found myself with such a son? Where would poetry have been then?

"Who's his father, Kath?" I asked.

"That," she said, "I do not know. But come and see us, Kai, for old time's sake."

Maybe I'd have gone but things moved quickly as they do in the spring. One morning he wasn't in the taxi that brought the children with special needs to us. He'd been taken to hospital in the middle of the night. In the class, we made a card for him. The children wrote poems and made paintings of eggs, nests, birds.

Fly back soon, little bird, they wrote.

I took the children's gifts to him. He was curled up in the great hospital bed, a tiny fragile wild thing hooked up to drips and tubes and electrodes. His breath was shallow. Tiny squeaks escaped from him. I sat with silent Kath. Robin's eyes moved rapidly behind their lids. I found myself trying to imagine what kind of wilderness he saw before him, what kind of wilderness he'd ever seen.

Kath took my hand and held it for a while.

"It's so strange," I said.

"You always said that," she whispered. "That things were strange."

"Did I?"

"Yes, in the old days. And you always said you'd go off travelling and never return."

Did I? I didn't remember telling her anything like that.

"But it *is* strange," I continued. "It's like I've always somehow loved him."

She took her hand away.

"That's such a stupid thing to say, Kai."

We prepared for OFSTED. I gave the children scores and grades, created charts and lesson plans. I predicted learning outcomes. The Head Teacher told us that the school's success depended on every single one of us. Beyond the fence, machines moved and the earth was levelled.

One day, I found Sally Smith weeping at the window.

"Look what's happening, sir," she said. "It's far too early, sir."

Bulldozers roared. Birds spiralled above the building site's dust. A huge billboard showed pale houses stretching across green hillsides beneath the sun.

There was no resistance.

"Maybe," I said, "when it's all over we should create a garden in the school grounds."

"A wild garden," she said. "We'll have a pond and wild flowers and…"

I saw the Head Teacher looking through the door.

"Yes. It will be lovely. Come on, Sally, back to your work now."

Robin died in the night before the inspection began. I didn't tell the children until the end of the first day. All day long, they'd been so good, so hardworking, so focussed. Their grief was a kind of liberation.

"We'll make that bliddy garden," said Sally. "It will be for Robin."

"Yes!" the others said.

She'd made another poster, stuck it on the wall.

DOWN WITH DEATH, it said.

"Yes!" they said.

They marched out into the streets weeping, holding each other tight, stamping the earth, yelling their useless fury at the empty sky.

The Inspectors asked me about the purposes of poetry. I didn't have their language. I said that poetry fed the soul, that it worked against the forces of destruction, that it filled the children with delight. I found myself laughing.

"They shall go flying," I said, "with musical speeches, High overhead, in the Tops of the beeches."

Much of the school was Outstanding. I was Grade 2: Good.

I left without giving notice. My career was over.

"You don't have what it takes, do you?" said the Head Teacher. "You have been using us, haven't you?"

On my final afternoon, the children chanted Stevenson and the classroom was merry with singing. They showed bright drawings of how their garden would be. Sally wrote me a poem that ended with the line, 'You have helped us to hatch.' Would I come back to see them again? they asked. I said that I would, knew that I wouldn't.

I cycled slowly away through Kath's street.

She came out to her gate.

"They say that he's been freed," she said. "They say he's in a better place."

"I'm so sorry," I whispered.

I stood by my bike and held her.

"But I think he's still here, Kai. In the early morning it's like I hear him, singing with all the birds."

I stayed with her for a while, and kissed her, then cycled to the city.

I hear him too, at the end of those wordless sleepless nights when the darkness fades and the light comes back and the music starts as it always does.

Yes, there he is, Robin Greed, and the souls of all the dear departed, singing back the day.

Philomel @ Nightingale

Jenni Fagan

In such a night, when every louder wind
Is to its distant cavern safe confined;
And only gentle Zephyr fans his wings,
And lonely Philomel, still waking, sings;

From 'A Nocturnal Reverie' by Anne Finch

I can only go out at night. It's okay. Don't @ me. The sun has her ways. I have mine. Her followers *like* to go out in daylight. I used to do that too but it began to happen less each year and month and then it was once a week and then every eighteenth day and then only for an hour and a minute per season. Now I don't go out during sundown – at all.

The hallowed released a statement.

It said – STOP: START: STOP: STOP: START again.

I don't talk to sun seekers. My only hope is that they will never know me.

No, I haven't gone to the police.

I won't say it again, don't @ me and don't try to ring my phone, it has long since died, I buried it by the mound where the cat went and the two of them can travel through infinity together. That cat loved the ringtone far more than I ever did and the sound of Candy Crush drove it wild, it was technologically connected whereas I – have always been a total technophobe.

The name plate on my front door has been gouged through until the letters are indecipherable.

It looks like a child's scribbles through the eyes on a magazine.

Still, the postman continues to deliver letters named to me – she has not mentioned the scars through my old name, I am not blind and she is an alcoholic and we like each other not at all. I don't blame her for doing two bottles per round. She told me quite bluntly one day that nobody would get mail without Shiraz, or at the very least Chianti, this makes it easier to know what to give her as a gift at Christmas and I'm sure that's what she intended by conveying her true conditions for attending work. Isn't it funny how we use the word blame when it comes to certain diseases? As if we have chosen certain illnesses out of weakness of character or some other personality flaw, rather than a genetically inherent propensity to such a thing?

Instead of another name I put up a postcard of an owl.

It looks down the lane.

All day!

It does it until the sun gives up and goes on her way.

Only at that point do I release my breath.

I have to wait her out with her heat and her sticky breath and I do, my house is like a fortress with every curtain closed and every shutter locked but it takes such a strain – all day of her stalking around. I know what she wants to do but I am never going to be a flame ball for her endless temper haze. Even when she feigns insipid white blankness she can't tempt me across the threshold. Her garish tendrils probe around the outside of my house, unfurl up towards the curtains, dance around on the path, wilt the poppies. Meanwhile I have taken to laying down star-shaped on the cool flagstones in my kitchen, seeking only the certainty of their touch on my skin. By that point she can't even tell if I am still breathing. Her flame skirt always flounces over the hill in the end. I don't even go near the door until I am sure that there is not even her finger left to point at me through the apple trees – I will never have it in me to trust that parch making, throat drying, skin ageing, attention guzzling, garishly tendrilled – fluster muppet of the blue azure.

It's what she is, and she knows it.

Once she is gone!

I begin to ease up, stretch out my legs, I might have my first glass of water then some time later, each night – I check conditions.

If they are wrong I do not leave the house at all.

Right now the hours have passed long enough in their procession through time and the garden is waiting.

I'm a minor figure.

Yet, how it still wants me.

I have no sister, she has no husband, I revoked all my other names.

You may call me Fi.

They say it is only the males who sing so what is this song that waits through all of the other horrible goings on in the world – waits – every second of every second – until it has its chance to pour out of me?

Not quite yet!

Tonight conditions are as good as they can be.

All hurricanes are otherwise diverted and no cracking of the earth and sinkholes gaping elsewhere and only the gentlest zephyr to caress the overhung green boughs by the river and the moon coming to carefully lay dewdrops upon fresh grass and each blade will feel so perfect beneath my bare feet.

There are four bolts on the door.

An alarm system to decode and a creak as I pull the old handle and look down the garden path.

Foxgloves.

Glow-worms.

Woodbind.

Bramble-rose.

In twilight they take to their stage with the totality of strangers, the fox glove paler than she was in her day, the smells of earth which receded from the burnt goddess now come out to find their way under deep, deep blue skies, they begin to scent the shadows.

What ancient light!

I step out.

One bare foot first and my skin adjusts to the soothing virtue of night – she has waited, for me, unlike my sister who turned first her face, then her heart and lays still with a husband who has left my body scarred.

I did not call the police.

Who even turns to them now?

Especially women, what is the point?

That is the sadness.

Hallowed strangers Lord themselves above us all – strung up in the newspapers like each one is a sun to blaze us back down into inertia and acceptance of their deceit. They can release all the statements they like because those of us who do not go out in daylight anymore know – at some point they will even come after night, the last thing to freely belong to us. There is such solace from seeking out loose nightmares, standing (as I do now) at the edge of fields watching horses glide through the gloom in the far distant corner, they could be any kind of great hulking shape – a dragon – or a tank – it is only the gentle sound as they clop onto a harder piece of ground allows them to reassemble themselves into a more familiar form. I wouldn't have minded if they had been great dragons come to tell a woman who no longer knows how to display her name – to hop on – the hay out there is heaped like an upside down cone of ice in some other life and no doubt there are mice burrowed inside it, congregating and mournful.

You can tell me not to be sedate but this world has viced us all in the great jaws of her poison.

Hope must only be encouraged – when she can be held.

It is such a night for things illicit and vital – I can hear curlews away down by the shore chattering after midnight, the long curves of their bills a silhouette by which waves cease to falter. The partridge has found a patch of ground to line with grass and every two days she lays her clutch (fifteen to twenty eggs) for fifty-five days she prays there shall be no heavy rain (eggs hatch in twenty-three) and leave their nest only days old and the joy of her heart must be hidden whilst all across the country men as tyrants sleep – easy – on silk – on cotton – on the arm of a woman who once spent time in a womb before me.

There is no justice and I am less trusting of the law than I am of the sun these days.

This morning the hallowed released a statement: it said – you voted in what you voted in, now is not a time to grow faint of heart – *we give you all we are – we tell you all we know* – and meanwhile we cannot go out to march because the word was clear: STOP: STOP: START: START: PAUSE. START: DON'T @ US the HALLOWED *we left in helicopters – we are no longer here*. My sister hates her husband yet she lays by him because she thinks it makes her more safe. She has married delusion. I'll only get her free if I kill him. I don't have the hands for it. She lies to herself and beside him, at least in some way, also, to protect me.

We'd go to the escape agencies but they are no longer funded.

Leave my mind!

Silence my musings!

I know a truth that is far too high to be touched by those far too indecent to ever be sorry.

The world is our garden.

Go out in her at night and ask her this…

Where would she bury the hallowed?

How cool is it under her earth?

My rage is disarmed by one thing only as I return through the grass and then down the path and back through the house and out the back door – to where the skin of my hurt has grown feathered.

I only half climb up the branches, feet turning to claws as they do.

Now I am pure.

I have a whole planet spread itself out below me – as I reach the tip of a Douglas fir.

Tilt back my throat and open my wings.

With all I have in my soul – I sing! I sing to all those others who don't cross their doors for fear of disease, or dismay, or denial and the debacle of law makers from the sun god – who let the good and the great and the meek and the plain and the honest and the funny and the righteous and the loved and the unloved – have fear lace their every waking day. I sing in deference to all those who try – unseen. I sing to my sister that she may not lay beside that man forever. I sing to my postmistress fitful in her sleep. I sing to the shore and I sing to the city – to the empty businesses and even emptier courts – I sing to mourn the fateful decisions of the hallowed – don't they know – there are treetops from which you can clearly look out at the whole world – up here it is possible to see – all things can be changed!

The impenetrable joy of living…

I revoke here and now all those things given to me that I did not want or ask for, the things my sister's husband called me, the things he did – until he left a legacy of pain in the heart and mind and atoms of a nightingale… who has ceased to have time anymore for day.

I sing in my tree to the garden of all night.

I sing to all the nights.

I sing to the heart of my sister so that she might remember she does not need a phone to ever call me and it doesn't matter if the agencies are closed and the hallowed have said every thought and deed must be shown under the brightest of daylight – she can find me in the garden.

It is my truth, it is my place, where the song in me flies in the face of sorrow.

I sing to a world where no child should ever again have to lower their gaze – I sing until I feel her reaching out for me – morning – pursuing her moment – to break – the spell of the song I am singing, in a garden where all things are true, where we are not at the mercy of the hallowed or the cold light of days endless – pursuit.

The Idler

Hannah Lavery

An idle lingerer on the wayside's road,
He gathers up his work and yawns away;
A little longer, ere the tiresome load
Shall be reduced to ashes or to clay.

No matter if the world has marched along,
And scorned his slowness as it quickly passed;
No matter, if amid the busy throng,
He greets some face, infantile at the last.

His mission? Well, there is but one,
And if it is a mission he knows it, nay,
To be a happy idler, to lounge and sun,
And dreaming, pass his long-drawn days away.

So dreams he on, his happy life to pass
Content, without ambitions painful sighs,
Until the sands run down into the glass;
He smiles – content – unmoved and dies.

And yet, with all the pity that you feel
For this poor mothling of that flame, the world;
Are you the better for your desperate deal,
When you, like him, into infinitude are hurled?

'The Idler' by Alice Moore Dunbar-Nelson

Sixteen days past your due date. Each morning, waking up like it was Christmas, only to be told it was Christmas Eve. All that endless waiting. Och! I should've known. Right from your first lazy kick.

They say you're the spit of your dad. Those Irish green eyes. That spattering of freckles – but your dad is never still like you are. He never stops. He's always up to his neck in a new project. He's honestly never happier than when he's fully immersed. My sweet man. Our jack of all trades, our master of none.

Your first summer he took our small empty garden and filled it with four raised vegetable beds, a mass of raspberry canes and two apple trees. I dug in the summer bulbs for us but this garden was to be utilised, every inch, ready for your weaning. He sweated and held his breath for you. Waiting for your next move and your next.

And that first year and maybe that second he mistook you for his very own. His double. When did he realise?

When was the first time he said pay attention? Certainly by six you'd shown yourself.

It's coming on noon and he is quietly raging now. Furiously turning the soil and weeding the beds. I tell him that that soil will never yield. It's a heavy clay, see? Compacted by all these identical compact homes.

'Just wake your son, will ye.'

He grumbles, loud enough for me to hear. Fourteen and you're definitely *my* son now. He still fights the soil but not you. He gave you up to the fairies years ago. 'I'll go,' I say. But I don't storm up to you, instead I'm sort of ambling, has your dreaming taken hold in me? Sometimes, I think it was you that shaped me.

—

And when did that begin? On that quiet walk home from the chemist to our flat? When I left your dad pacing in the kitchen? While I waited for the results of you, staring at the pregnancy test, sat on the edge of the bath? After I knew? When I stayed with the news of you for another three minutes?

Son, you took us over like a cuckoo.

We, who have rushed our whole lives, our whole marriage, run from next thing, to glorious next thing. One quick dash. Minutes. Surely, it's only minutes since we started? Yet you seem to have all the time, like you took it from us. Living all our time on a go-slow, while we live what's left at full pelt.

And you know? I can't remember if you were ever easy to wake. Each school day, each holiday trip had to have a lead-up of at least an hour. It wasn't that you were averse to a change in the plans or to the new adventure, it was that you wanted it on your terms, at your own pace – it was your time and you would take it, but this long lying in? I mean, I know it's your age. The teenage boy, it's not wilful, not deliberate, yet?

And I am reluctant to nag you. To knock on your door. My Indian grandmother used to bang pots and hoover outside my bedroom door if I ever dared to sleep in. I won't do that. Not because I am nicer or more tolerant but because I am afraid. I fear you've grown too fond of dreaming. I worry I won't be able to reach you.

He thinks about dragging you out of your bed.

'All this hard work for him to walk around life like it's not happening.'

I don't respond to this. I have run out of ways to explain you. It's generational. That's what he thinks.

'They don't have the same work ethic. The same drive.'

But how can we blame you for that – what's there to work for anymore?

'Just wake your son, will ye.'

He knows that hurts me.

'Listen love, there is no need to act like that.'

And that? Well that does it. There'll be no rescuing the day now. And he thinks I can't hear him. Oh! My love. I see him and his father in you but there is none of the same fire and none of that sticking power, that getting-stuck-in power. There was the violin, the swimming, the judo, the scouts. All took up and then put down.

'It's just not me.'

'I can't be bothered.'

And then there was the football, and you know? He's right. It's a prime example.

All that summer, you were football mad. He got you all the gear and signed you up to the local kids' team. First practice and there we were on the sidelines, proud as anything, and you go and spend the whole hour sitting in the goals. As deaf to the coach as the goal posts, sat like you were waiting on a sandwich. Cute? Of course. Hilarious? Of course but that lackadaisical attitude went on for weeks, months, years now. Flinching away from the ball. Running in the wrong direction. Wandering off for a drink halfway through a match.

He said, 'listen son, this is not for you.'

'I like it,' you said.

What could we do?

'I love it,' you say.

'Ten pounds in subs, for him to be sat on the bench,' he says.

If you're happy, what's the harm? And he gets that, he does, but he says, it's a prime example.

'I have nothing to work with. He's like this bloody soil.'

And forgive me but for a moment, I agree, then I tell him that he's more like you than he cares to admit.

'Whit?' he says.

Later he complains that I have put thoughts in his head. We fear our faults will show up in our kids, I tell him. We become hyper-vigilant to them and he starts to question himself, he does, but then it's the inevitable: 'I'm not going back on what I said.'

He's all for the forward momentum of life, it's maybe why I fell for him. It's a race, he would tell you. You have to try and understand him, he wants so much for you. His parents wanted more for him. It's the immigrant thing, of course, he would tell you, although it's not really that. It's not that at all.

When you were wee, you were always toddling off – with this adorable drunken walk – and he would always follow. Those long sweet days you spent together, full of all these tiny wee moments. That way he would crouch down to you every time you were stopped by something.

'What's this, daddy?'

'Look at this, daddy?'

Your hand picking up a fallen leaf to show him and only him. Gentle over a slug in your path. Chasing the crisp packet caught by the wind. Once you insisted on holding on to this lost red sock. Your dad called it Marty, took it home and washed it for you. The two of you would spend an hour walking ten minutes. Time just… it just moved differently. It wound down. It stretched out.

You were his wondrous beautiful boy. He pitied and mocked the parents with their dull and predictable kids. He went with every slow meandering step of yours, followed your gaze, followed your lead and he never minded. He didn't mind it all. To others you were just stumbling about, speaking baby nonsense but he understood every single word of you.

'Are you listening to the birds?'

Do you remember wanting to learn how to match the song to the bird? I rushed out and got you that book – remember? I am pretty sure you didn't read it. I found it later in your dirty washing. I had made it another opportunity for learning.

Every day is a school day!

You just wanted to listen to the birds.

'I am not your project. My life is not a reflection of your great choices.'

You said this to me like it was just another thing you said. You think you see us so clearly – don't you? With our early morning rituals and new regimes posted to the fridge. A quest for perfection, you called it.

He says it's your age, but then he also says you've always been at an awkward age. 'A spoiled brat,' he rails at me but not to you – to you…

'We'll show them.'

Made for great things, we used to whisper to you, but not recently. You're not useless. You're not a waste of space. Please, we don't think that – not really? Not often. It's just… you don't believe that we're meant to live like this – do you?

He says it's your age.

Though now he's starting to say it's your generation. Tries to understand the politics of the millennial. To be honest, I am not sure that's it, and you're far too young to be a millennial.

Life's too short for all this, you said, Exactly, he replied, and I said, you must make your own mark. You didn't bother to argue with us but you are not interested in making marks – are you? You just want to... I don't know. I don't know what you want to do. Nothing we'd recognise. Listen to the birds. Not for credit, but because they're singing.

At the beginning of the year, Dad and I decided that mindfulness was our new thing. Yes, I know. Classes were booked. Three months of the inevitable obsession followed. Your dad was evangelical.

'Live in the moment, son.'

'You must try it, son.'

'Change your life, son.'

You watched us, in that way you watch us, as we woke up even earlier to squeeze in our meditation before we got at you for your lack of ambition.

What must you have thought of us?

I suppose, it's just the way of things, that we end up ridiculous to our own children; and this whole thing of being really present, well, you've been showing us all along – haven't you?

I'm not sure when you became such a problem.

'Son?'

I've been sneaking in like this, to look at you sleeping, since you were a baby. Pushing the closed door open to get that precious wee peep. I have become so skilful in not waking you.

'Son?'

They say, you can find calm anywhere. I've always found it watching you. Listening to the very breath of you. We mothers find it hard to let go, or so they tell us. I am not sure. I think we always know you're separate from us. We get that from the first heartbeat, so different from our own. We are always preparing to let our children go.

And I am no good at telling you about all that you've given to me. I feel at constant war with all the hope I have for you, and all that you are – which is now. Right now. You tell me over and over not to wish you away. I watch you dreaming there, my love. And I know the truth of that but from your waking to your sleeping again I feel compelled to compel you. To make your mark. You don't need to though – do you? You know life, how to live it, so much better than we ever did.

'Sweetheart?'

'Mum?'

'Come join us in the garden.'

'Now?'

'When you're ready, son.'

The Garden

Jessie Greengrass

For the doubling of flowers is the improvement of the gardner's talent.
For the flowers are great blessings.
…

For flowers are good both for the living and the dead.
For there is a language of flowers.
For there is a sound reasoning upon all flowers.
For elegant phrases are nothing but flowers.
For flowers are peculiarly the poetry of Christ.
For flowers are medicinal.
For flowers are musical in ocular harmony.
For the right names of flowers are yet in heaven. God make gard'ners better nomenclators.

From 'Jubilate Agno' by Christopher Smart

From the moment that the first bell rings I wish to be in the garden, but there is no hurrying. We rise and dress, and we go in silence to the first congregation. When the second bell rings, we go to the refectory. For breakfast it is porridge as always, spooned from the great iron pot sitting on its table at the end of the room where the big window, on fine mornings, sheds light upon it. I can't see Marguerite. She has chosen to sit behind me, which is a message. Meaning: I have something to say to you. Meaning: It is too important to be prefaced by looks.

The third bell is the sign for us to stand and go to our jobs. This we do also in silence. Or, rather, this we do without speaking; because although we strive for silence, yet we cannot help but make noise, which is a lesson in itself
 -A lesson in what?

Marguerite might ask, before supplying her own answer, which would be along the lines of

-A lesson in futility;

but I would say it is a lesson in the value of reaching. That is, of reaching beyond ourselves. And so, in place of silence, there is the noise of thirty women, moving in their various directions.

There is the noise of chairs, scraping across flags.

There is the noise of crockery.

There is the noise of coughing, which is the noise of Eleanor Francis, who caught a cold at Whitsun which has settled on her chest.

There is the noise of feet, which is the noise of movement: of progress outwards, into the day. Of my own feet, their soft flap-flap-flap as I walk along the passage towards the door. And past the door, the garden.

The rule is that besides the conversation hour we should not talk, but there are more ways to pass a message than with the mouth.

There are the eyes, which might be lifted or lowered. There is the way a woman walks, the set of her shoulders, the turn of her head.

Then, too, there are the eyebrows, which might be cocked or set, and there are nods, there are shrugs. There are gestures which mean Please; Sorry; By all means you first; or, I was about to eat that apple which you have picked up, it is my own apple and you must give it back.

There is a particular way of turning the inside of one's wrist outwards which means: We will talk later.

For my own part, I find the complexities of such a system joyful. The restraint is a problem which must be solved, in silence, amongst ourselves. It encourages complicity, which is both care and warmth.

-Isn't that rather missing the point of it, though? Marguerite says.

-Isn't that ignoring the part of it which is about control? Which is about the control *of us*?

-Marguerite,

I say, when the subject comes up,

-It's not that I enjoy being unable to say whatever comes into my head whenever I want to. But Marguerite. Think of that moment in the morning. Think of that moment first thing in the morning, when all you can hear is scraping and clanking and coughing and clattering and your own thick feet against the flagstones. Think of how it is like an itching inside your skull, an irritation, and think how it is then when you pass through the door into the garden. It is so open, Marguerite. It is wide open and the air is balm, the leaves rubbing against the branches are balm, and the rain too sometimes, which does not flap or clack but drips and runs and splashes. These things are like a kind hand laid on a forehead. And you wouldn't have thought to hear them if it hadn't been for what went before. Marguerite,

I say

-think what joy it is to be in the garden,
and Marguerite, unusually, says nothing.

I would not want to give a misleading impression. Marguerite is not lacking in consideration. She is good, both in herself and as a gardener.

No one but Marguerite can inhabit the garden with such completeness.

No one but Marguerite can know with such certainty the names of all the things that sprout, or with such deftness prune the branches of the plum trees, seeing in advance where each new shoot will choose to grow.

No one is more gentle. No one more kind.

I have seen her sift through turned soil for worms to move them to a suitable location.

I have seen her leave out straw for the birds, so that they will not pull up the lawn to build their nests.

I have seen her hold a blown rose between her cupped fingers, and cut it, and hand it to me, so that when I take it from her its petals fall like joy into my lap.

This morning Marguerite is ahead leaving the refectory, and so by the time I have gone into the garden, she is already there. She stands in the grass, her hands on her hips, staring downwards. Her skirt is knotted up around her thighs. Her feet are bare.

-Marguerite,
I say,
-for heaven's sake, where are your boots,

but Marguerite, who doesn't look up, not even for a moment, says nothing at all about her boots. Instead, she says,

-Bloody hell, have you seen what the snails have done to these hostas.

We stand side by side, staring down at the uneven lacework that is all that's left of yesterday's long leaves, and I am just about to say,

-Look on the bright side, at least they haven't had at the lettuces,

when Marguerite says,

-I have been thinking that I want to leave.

It is true that we should not be talking, not even in the garden, but surely the rules for outside are different. Outside, we are open to the sky. Outside, we move beneath the wide eye of the sun. Outside, in the garden, we are no different to the birds in the branches, and so we let our voices mingle with those of the sparrow and the pheasant, the blackbird and the swift which screams as it races in company around the house. In the garden, I reason to Marguerite, we are commensurate with these beings, and so how can our noise, and not theirs, be wrong? It is only indoors that we might be considered furtive.

-Or,

says Marguerite,

-And here's a thought. Is it because no one can actually hear us, out here?

Today we must plant out the cabbages, which jostle together in their seedbeds. My job is the preparation of the soil. I fetch compost from the heap and dig it into the ground. When I am done, Marguerite will lift the young plants one by one and bring them to their final places. While she waits, she weeds around the carrots.

-You could,

I say,

-Bring the matter up at a meeting. You could ask to be transferred. Released, even.

Marguerite shakes her head, her face still turned towards the soil.

But—

I say.

-No.

A blackbird that has been pecking at the turned earth hops away, affronted by the loudness of her voice. We watch it. At a certain distance it stops and turns to glare at us, before beginning again to explore the possibilities of the soil.

-Listen,

she says, quietly now, so that indeed I must listen.

-I don't need permission. I don't want my freedom granted me. How can anyone give what is already mine?

She sits back on her heels and looks at me.

-It's not the same for me as it is for you.

-In what way?

I ask.

-In what way, Marguerite, is it not the same?

All is in order in the garden. Underneath the canopy of the willow tree, Marguerite and I lie, side by side. Her arm supports my head, mine curves around her waist. I breathe into her neck. I say,

-I didn't choose to come here, any more than you did.

Marguerite takes her time to answer. She strokes my cheek. She says,

-It isn't about what we chose, it is about what we have found. You have found a home here. The confines make you safe. The rules, too. You are made safe inside them. I have heard,

she says,

-how you cry out in your sleep. I know how afraid you have been.

-And you?

I ask.

-Have you not been afraid, Marguerite?

-Well,

she answers,

-If I have, then I am no less so for being inside these bloody walls.

The tenth bell is the last of the day, marking the time when we should go to our beds and, faces washed, clothes neatly folded, lie down to be buried in darkness, counting our breaths out into that empty space which sleep will not fill. This is the bell I dread. Tonight, though, it rings and I do not obey it. Tonight, instead of going to the dormitory, I follow Marguerite into the kitchen. She has a knapsack – I could not say where she got it – and into it we place a loaf of bread, a pat of butter, some apples, a cheese. Our heads are close together.

 -Marguerite,

I say, and although we are indoors I speak boldly, because what I need to tell her is important and I will risk what might come through any cracks my errancy creates.

 -Marguerite, you are wrong. It is not freedom and nor is it peace that I have found in the garden. It is you.

Hand in hand we go out through the door and we walk along the path until we reach the wall. For a moment, Marguerite turns to me and comes very close, resting her forehead against mine, and then she steps away again, hitches up her skirt, begins to climb. It is too dark to see her, but I can hear the sound of her feet as they find leverage, and after that I can hear the absence of sound as she reaches the top of the wall. I think she is finding her balance, up there, and for a moment I think that I might follow her; but after all she is not so very wrong. The garden is my home.

There is the sound of an owl, hooting.

There is the sound of Marguerite shifting the weight of her bag upon her back.

There is the sound of her jumping, and then the sound of her hitting the earth on the other side of the wall, and I listen for what will come next – for the sound of her feet, running, which will be the sound of loss, of desolation; which will be the sound of being left behind – but instead, through the darkness, where there should be rupture there is the sound of singing, and because I know this song I too begin to sing it, and for a while there is no other sound but this: Marguerite's voice and my own, raised, rejoicing.

*He Wishes for the Cloths
of Heaven*

PK Lynch

Had I the heavens' embroidered cloths,
Enwrought with golden and silver light,
The blue and the dim and the dark cloths
Of night and light and the half-light,
I would spread the cloths under your feet:
But I, being poor, have only my dreams;
I have spread my dreams under your feet;
Tread softly because you tread on my dreams.

'He Wishes for the Cloths of Heaven' by W.B. Yeats

Hello there, Mammy. Don't wake up, sure, I'm far too early, so I am. I was sitting at your old sewing machine in the dark of my bedroom, worrying about waking the lads, when I just wondered what the hell I was doing *there* when I could be sitting right beside you doing it *here*. Sure, haven't I fingers, I thought, and aren't they a sight more transportable than your old Singer? So I put everything in a big bag, left a note for John telling him where I've gone, and look now – here I am and it's not even six o'clock. There was a wee confusion at the main door on account of the hour but they know me here now – a wink and a smile and they let me through.

Well. Are you ready for the big reveal? I'm no seamstress, as you well know, but the thought sprouted and wouldn't be ignored. It's not quite what I set out to do. I should have googled the best method. It all seemed quite straightforward as I started out but like so many things in my life – pay attention, Mammy, because I'm making a *confession* here – the further in I got, the bigger a mess I made. You should have seen the look John gave me when he saw it. I can't abide sympathy from a man, even if he is my husband, so I threw the whole thing out and started again. I used Google this time, I can tell you, and I quickly found I'd never have the patience to do it properly. It'd be one of those jobs that lie around for years waiting to be finished. It'd probably end up in my own child's loft after they've cleared out *my* house, you know what I mean? So I took matters into my own hands and it's not so much a patchwork quilt as... what would you call it... a memory blanket. I'm going to sit nice and quiet now and get on with it. You keep snoozing.

It's a lovely fleecy blanket I'm using. One of Oliver's. What I've done is cut out lots of fabric squares, quite large, larger than they said to online, and I've taken smaller squares and I've cut them up into shapes. Then the shapes go on the bigger squares and the bigger squares go on the blanket and stitch, stitch, stitch until what you have is a single, complete, personalised memory blanket.

There's an apple for the tree we planted to remember Daddy. Something a bit like a spaniel for Toby. Well, I think it looks like him anyway. All your babies, of course, all three of them in a square of their own. Just the initials, Mammy, portraits are a bit beyond me. P for me, S for Sarah and V for Violet. And a wee crucifix for Violet. I placed it beside Daddy's square and Toby's. That felt right. Funny how the saddest events make the strongest memories. But then I thought hard about all the good stuff, you know? Like your camper-van trip around Canada which, to be honest Mammy, we all considered a bit random, but good on you. I drew a rough outline of a camper-van on a piece of calico, blue calico to be specific, and I cut it out and added it to everything else. A little bit of white stitching for the windows, black for the wheels and that. Keep you motoring alright. It looks ace. A shape on a square, on a blanket, repeat. Sure, a life is more than a bundle of sad memories.

The memories fade anyway. They seem to go in reverse order, little puffs of cloud blown away until everything's gone but the hazy past. A different place altogether. A world before I was even thought of. I feel locked out. Not that I'm offended. Besides, stories are coming out of the woodwork in the most unexpected of ways. People I never even met are getting in touch. Telling me the stories you can't. Some of them I'm sworn not to repeat because of course they're not just stories, they're people's lives. The life you looked after all those years ago, the woman you took in and never said a word to me about. She came to see me. I'm not sure exactly how she knew about your situation. Anyway, she told me all about it. How you treated her like a sister when others shunned her. Made her dresses as she grew. Best dressed fallen woman for miles, she said. She wants you to know you were right about keeping it. Her daughter's a surgeon now, isn't that great? Helping people. Saving them. All down to you. And to think I almost never knew. No matter. I'll tell Oliver about it, and maybe one day he'll tell his sons or daughters, and maybe that way your kindness will live on.

Oliver. That boy bawled his head off when he arrived in the world. The doctors laughed about it. But the moment he heard my voice he *quietened*, and everything else – all my pain, all my fear – just faded away, like the whole terrifying business had happened to some other person in some other place. We were bonded in that moment. I felt it. The whole room did, you could feel it. I'll never forget that. Such a silence. Oliver's eyes on mine. We looked into each other, and our souls were forever bonded.

Do all mothers feel that way about their children? Or can it skip and emerge sometimes only with the grandchildren? I've seen you with Oliver. How you stroke his soft, round cheeks when you think no one's looking. Who could blame you? The wispy fur of his eyebrows are as perfect as anything I've seen, that tiny dip beneath his bottom lip – God, I can't not put my pinky finger in it. The warmth of his head, his smell. "That's your life over now," Sarah said, my ever-supportive little sister, but the wise person in the room said, "no. That's your life just beginning." Well, they do say that happens at forty, though I don't think geriatric motherhood's what they had in mind. Geriatric feckin' motherhood. I'll admit I'm more tired. Sure, it's difficult to do anything at all, much less get out of bed when I don't have to, but somehow these past few weeks I've managed in the mornings to tear myself away. I tried to carry the feel of him with me to the sewing machine. I needed to be calm. What a monster that thing is. I never tamed it. But I maybe began to feel a little bit of a helping hand beside me, because even though I'd no clue what I was doing, the stitches somehow appeared on the fabric like magic. The thread did its job. It ran through. Held everything together. It held everything together.

This square here, it's got my actual blood in it, can you believe? I pricked myself with the damn needle and my blood oozed from a tiny wee hole – a wound invisible to the naked eye – soaking into the white silk. It reminded me of that fairy tale, actually. And that makes *who* the wicked stepmother, exactly?

Just joking.

Do you know there's a power to being awake in a room when a person's sleeping. When a person's lying there so small in the bed, their hair all fuzzed up, soft and thin like a spider web sticking about their head. The way a mouth can gape and glisten. A strain around the eyebrows giving an earnestness to the face. Like a person is concentrating. Sticking to the shadows of their life. Choosing the darkness.

We need light in here. I'm just twisting the blinds now – oh, it's lovely. Warm. Golden. Somehow it helps you breathe, light like this. It's lit up the wall opposite me.

The gallery wall. Very fancy, Mother. That picture of you as a little girl with your brothers, sitting atop a hay bale in granda's farm. Grinning like loons, I'm hard pushed to say which of you looks cheekiest.

How many times have I said that now.

"Hard pushed to say which of you looks cheekiest." Your reply is always the same, except for the odd time it isn't, when you look at me like I've betrayed you, because all of a sudden you know we've had this conversation a million times before and I'm too stunned by your fleeting comprehension to make the most of the moment before you slip away again, and then we're back to it, me chasing you like I'm still a little girl, only now it's your memories I'm trying to catch, Mammy, you and all those memories of the time before I was born, before I was even thought of, the same ones all the time going round and around like the present doesn't even exist, like I don't even exist. This is it now, this is the pattern. It's new but it's ingrained, and we'll repeat it just as the moon rises and the tides flow. We'll repeat it till we wear away. Become something else altogether.

Well.

Stitching away.

I daresay Foghorn Mary will swing by shortly with her dulcet tones. That woman would be better suited in a double act with a lighthouse than as a care worker in a nursing home. I mean – I know I'm hardly sitting here whispering to you myself, Mammy, but that's different. You know my voice well enough. Sure, you've been blocking it out for years.

Well.

This blanket here. So far we've got: weddings, graduations, daughters, a cross for Violet, an apple for Daddy – Toby, of course, woof woof. Sarah's kids, the Canada trip… a, a what would I call this now, an *interesting* interpretation of the drama faces, what are they called? Oh yes. Comedy and Tragedy. Oh, poor Jean Smithers in the village hall, keeling over like that in the middle of *Hello, Dolly*. What a way to go. Hello Dolly, goodbye Jean Smithers. At least she had a fancy frock on at the time. Year after year, all that effort and everyone knew the costumes were the best part of it.

Feck. I'm missing the most obvious thing of all here. A bobbin, or a spool of thread, or a measuring tape or something. I'll do you a bobbin. Of course I will.

I'm stitching memories here. No loose threads, no unravelling.

A shape on a square, on a blanket, repeat.

Pile them up. A great big patchwork of memories.

I can't believe I only just thought of a bobbin.

What else am I missing? A shape on a square, on a blanket, repeat. Stitching together your life, holding your memories together in the one place. Get it on the blanket. Get it all on. Everything.

But how? How is everything supposed to fit onto it? I'm waking earlier and earlier to do this, in the hopes of giving it and seeing real honest-to-God joy for what

– let's face it, Mammy – will possibly, probably, definitely, may be the last gift I give you. But it'll never be done. It'll never do.

What about all those stories I'll never know? All the things you said and did, all the friends you made, the people you loved. All the good you did. How you made us feel. Getting all that on a blanket? By the time I finish, I'll have forgotten the beginning. By the time I finish, it'll be impossible to tell it's a blanket at all.

I suppose that's alright. It'll just be a gigantic, scruffy spool of life.

I'll lay it over you now, Mammy. The good, the bad, and the messy. Doesn't it feel nice? This section here, this is the church you married Daddy in. I used blue and green thread for the stained glass windows. I like to think you're still inside, and somehow I'm in there with you. We're on tiptoes, trying to peek out, trying to catch all the colours of the sea and the hills and sky. But we can't. We can't see anything beyond but we don't even care because the light is so lovely. It falls all over us. Enjoy the light, Mammy. Dream of it. I'll keep stitching away.

Carpe Diem

Cathy Forde

sapias, vina liques et spatio brevi
spem longam reseces. Dum loquimur, fugerit invida
aetas: carpe diem quam minimum credula postero.

be wise, strain the wine – as time is short,
scale back your hopes to the brief span of life.
While we are talking, jealous time flies away.
And so, seize the day, and trust little in tomorrow.

from Ode, Book 1 Poem 11 by Horace

Another dippy present from my sister-in-law.

Optional message in the special greetings box. *Belated happy birthday, God knows you need pampering!*

A wellness retreat this time. *Not* Carol's thing. Probably a regift. What *I* need? My finger hovered over my phone. What *I* need is for you to send yourself here in person. For you to be me for a day, a night, a month...

I chose a string of emojis to ping back to Carol: hearts, thumbs up, praying gratitude hands, more hearts.

Carol's voucher was destined to expire in the kitchen drawer of useless stuff alongside her other conscious-salving gestures. Pedicures, hot stone massages, facials... Like beauty treatments could transform anything. Even if I *could* find the time.

Or was I just being sour?

I really try not to be sour.

'You're being a bit sour, mum. Auntie Carol means well,' Charlie talked me down on the phone. And you *do* need something like this. Posh overnight in Corrie Castle?'

'But it's a night away. It's not like Carol's offering to—'

'What date suits, mum?'

'Listen. Charlie you are *not* coming up from Bristol...'

Charlie came up from Bristol. Took the train so he could work on it. He'd drop me at Corrie Bay because he'd need the car for Joe.

'Good excuse for a blow along the seafront anyway, isn't it?' Charlie reached across the handbrake to pat his dad. 'Maybe an ice-cream?'

From the back seat I watched Joe turn his head from the suggestion. Stare out the passenger window. The wipers beat time.

'Remember you'd bring us down here, dad?' Charlie's cheeriest voice punctured the silence. 'Poor mum's always been stuffed in the back.'

I helped Charlie out.

'And Susan sticking her head out the window, Joe?'

'Susan not,' Joe mumbled.

'Say again, dad?' Charlie seized. 'You said something.'

I had to throw my lovely boy a lifebelt: 'I think dad means Susan's not here.'

Joe was right too: Susan not. After last Christmas my daughter decided this was all too difficult. Her wee ones didn't understand what was wrong with Papa.

'Hey, dad, if Sooz had come, it would've been a proper *complete nightmare.*'

'You'd be driving and holding the sick bowl for Charlie,' I chipped in. 'Remember?'

When I squeezed Joe's shoulder, he wrenched away.

Did you see that, Charlie? That's what it's like. A *nightmare*, Susan? You think?

When we arrived at Corrie, I came round to Joe's door.

'Roll your window down.' I twirled my finger from behind the glass. Joe blinked out like he didn't know what he was looking at. Hands on his lap turning his cap over and over. Beside him, Charlie was staring at the side of his dad's face. Charlie's expression. His eyes. Jesus. I'd to catch myself. Inhale. Exhale.

If I didn't get moving, I'd be back in the car. In the driving seat.

'So I'll see you tomorrow, Joe. Charlie's on duty. Taking you for a curry.'

When I leaned in to my husband, his hand blocked my kiss, cheek arching away in rage and confusion.

'Mum, it's not duty. You just make the most of your break.' Charlie pulled the passenger door shut.

Before there was any Charlie or Susan, there was a day we came down here to Corrie Bay on the bus. Me and Joe. Hadn't been going out long. Couldn't keep our hands off each other. Couldn't stop smiling into each other's eyes, seeing our giddy, shiny selves reflected back. The way he looked at me. Kissed me, his finger smoothing back strands of my hair. Kissed me harder; longer, when some biddy sitting behind us started tutting. I didn't know anybody could make me feel so happy. But Joe did. *Real* Joe. He found the fun in everything. It was what I liked, then loved. In those golden years before silly jokes start grating on a marriage's novelty. Or get taken for granted.

I can still bring back the feeling of Joe's lips against my ear. Me laughing. Weak from wanting him.

'Too top notch for the likes of us, kiddo,' Real Joe would have been nudging his knee hard against mine if he'd checked into Corrie Castle with me today. Behind the reception this groomed and glossy girl attended in a designer version of a nurse's tunic. She greeted me in hushed tones with sparkling water and a Relaxation menu: Yin yoga, tai chi, reflexology... Therapies every link and care and social worker had been telling and telling me I really should make time for.

'You won't want to leave,' the designer tunic girl promised. She looked so put out when I insisted I could carry my own backpack to the room, I was tempted to confide it contained little more than fresh underwear and a nightie.

On Bach strings and the heady scent of stargazer lilies, I was wafted to my room in her wake. Beneath my feet the deep pile was a measure of the luxury of this place. In a bedroom that would take me all day to dust, lunch waited under a cloche. Champagne in an ice bucket, courtesy of Charlie.

This day, I realised, was actually mine. My only commitment a 'Mindfulness Walk' Carol had pre-booked for me as a treat. About an hour, I had.

In Paradise. To relax.

Relax?

A bath, I decided. I could hardly ignore the claw-footed giant in the bathroom, after all. Plus I couldn't recall when I'd last taken one. But no sooner was I chin-deep in perfumed bubbles than I had to come out.

It was Joe.

I know he wasn't there, but he was hovering. That sense of him. His needs. Wanting me to do something, like he always did as soon as I found a moment alone. He might as well have checked in.

At least – I dredged up one of the *recalibration strategies* from some positivity course for carers I'd thought was worse than useless at the time – at least this Mindfulness Walk would give me a decent stretch along the sands. It was a fine day for it too. Watery sun, and a brisk breeze, its salt sting recharging my depleted batteries with positive ions. Better than that, this was a rare chance to travel at my own speed, un-slowed by Joe's lagging gait. Both of us wanting to be elsewhere. He used to embrace the wind and the wet, but nowadays Joe took weather personally. Took the hump. I thought of Charlie. How was he coping with the man baby who possessed his dad's body?

How long had I spent in the lap of luxury and my thoughts were already circling back to duty? Back to guilt. Stop it, I told the woman in the mirror with the lines of worry etched deep round her mouth.

That other day-trip day – when Joe was still Joe – couldn't have been worse. Weather-wise, I mean. Rain sheeting off our noses, my hair hanging in wet ropes that I lashed at him in mock reproach.

'This is your idea of a hot date, Romeo?'

We walked the Corrie Sands anyway. Of course we did; we were in the crucible of *amour*. Daft with it. Heads pressed, arms clinging. Howling Blowin' In The Wind braced against the squall.

With its miles of hard packed sand on the Castle's doorstep, there for the pacing, not to mention the therapeutic whip of the waves' grey roar, I assumed I'd be retreading my previous lovestruck footsteps on this Mindfulness Walk. Whatever that was. Instead, I mustered at reception to be greeted by Jude, a woman in birdwatcher camouflage. Ages with myself, Jude was, if less harried-looking.

'So.' Leading me round the back of the castle, Jude set off inland through its grounds. At my kind of clip at least. We were well beyond the formal lawns before Jude paused beneath a willow tree. Small white cards dangled from the branches.

Be kind to yourself
Try to live in the moment
You are loved

I kinked my neck to read the twisting messages.

'Now.' Jude's voice was soft. Irish maybe. From one of the multiple pockets in her jacket, she fished out a small white card for me. A Corrie Castle pen.

'For later if you want to, But first, you follow me. We don't talk. You don't worry where you're going. Just slow down and let your mind breathe out its thoughts. In and out.'

Seriously?

Let my mind breathe out its thoughts.

Carol paid *extra* for this? If Jude heard me splutter, she didn't turn back. Slower than Joe-pace now, she processed into a dappled thicket. And, at first, I followed her.

That other time, when Joe and I belted, hand-in-chilled-hand, from Corrie beach and up the Castle driveway, it felt like the rain had seeped into the marrow of our bones. Old hotels like this, Joe was confident, would have kept a roaring fire going in the bar. Even in July. Not that he'd insider knowledge of hotels or bars. We'd dry and thaw nursing brandies because Joe said they were the boys for warming up. Not that he'd insider knowledge of spirits. The bar staff would take pity on two bedraggled day trippers. Fall for our fake student ids. They did neither; this was the days when the liveried doorman policed prospective clientele. I was so miserable, being turned out into the rain, that I could have wept. I didn't though. Got annoyed. Snarky. I was always getting annoyed with Joe; his irrepressible optimism.

Still am. Not at his optimism. That's history. Raging because he's gone but he's not and I'm left with what he's not. And because it's led to *this*.

Mindfulness walk?

My mind was full of *these* thoughts: that I was ridiculous, crunching overgrown woodland, watching my step. Itching to overtake this woman. What was wrong with the beach? I could power walk there. Fast. Far less exhausting than this keeping pace with someone else. Speed is my default setting; how I do anything for myself. It has to be. Time's not mine, save for snatched escapes while Joe sits in front of Pointless. While he fixes on the screen, out I go. Full tilt. Move so fast I can out-breathe the grief, you see. I never slow down. Daren't. Or else the thoughts seep in.

Like now. Here. Unexpectedly.

When the power leaves my legs, I have to reach for the nearest tree. Ragged panic catches my throat. As Jude wavers from view, her steady footsteps deal out a truth I will never outwalk: even here, in Paradise, the minutes of my life are counting off, synched to another's. Even here, I can never escape. Pointless to try.

Beneath a canopy of oak trees in full summer green I slump and weep for the first time in years. And weep. I don't know how long I am huddled there, but when my shudders are passed, I notice the sun is warming my face, shafting a route down to me through the branches above. Its light refracts the tears on my lashes, splitting them into rainbow threads. The threads dance and shimmer. A robin keeps his eye on me. Sparrows let me eavesdrop their chat and, before long, I find I am smiling.

And maybe it's the feel of my wet cheeks. Or maybe the smell of dank, soft earth. Of bark and foliage. But a lost memory surfaces.

That other time. Before Joe and I broke shelter from the Castle grounds for the bus back home, he pulled me under one of the trees on the grand driveway. Pressed into me, drying my face with his hands.

Joe's lips and even his tongue felt cold, as he murmured into my mouth, 'I'll try to make sure it doesn't get worse.'

Thank you – I tie my message card on a twig for the birds to ponder.

'Family commitments,' I tell the glossy girl when I leave the hotel, Charlie's champagne in my backpack. I check the time of the next bus, then call him. 'We'll drink it tonight after the curry,' I tell my son. Then I wait in the same shelter I'd huddled with Joe all those years back, his jacket round my shoulders. My head against his.

Before I went back to him, to Joe, I'd even managed my power walk on the beach.

And that was better than enough.

The Grey Eagle

Harry Josephine Giles

In a fair place
   Of whin and grass,
   I heard feet pass
   Where no one was.

I saw a face
   Bloom like a flower—
     Nay, as the rain-bow shower
   Of a tempestuous hour.

It was not man, nor woman :
   It was not human :
   But, beautiful and wild
   Terribly undefiled,
   I knew an unborn child.

                      'The Vision' by Fiona Macleod

From the desk of James Straiton
Taigh an Lochain, Eadar-dà-chaolas, Sutherland
on the sixth of July, 1905

My dear Charles,
It causes me the utmost regret to learn from your letter that you believe I have deceived you in the matter of Miss Malvina Mackay, with whom you have been in such frequent correspondence these past years. In these pages I have written, as I sit before the window of my study, pausing only to draw comfort from the sunlit view of my own little blue lochan, only such details as will set your mind at ease regarding the Gaelic poetess, she of the smooth brow of the *Clann Mhic Aoidh*, chronicler of all in these islands that is most alive and free. It is of course by my literary endeavours, dear Charles, that you and I first met, and so perhaps it is more than appropriate that it shall be through the work of my pen

that our acquaintance may be remade. My fond hope is that you will come to understand Miss Mackay's presence in both of our lives as none but the greatest blessing.

I begin with a memory. You will recall, of course, the spring you and I spent together in Venice as the days tumbled towards the century's close. If you would cast your mind back through the intervening years, back to that strangely sultry season when the rains refused to come; when we set aside our industrious pens to seek knowledge of the world beyond our scholarly labours; when each morning the proud voices of market traders mingled with the wicked cries of innumerable gulls; when as young men without direction we strolled together through the three thousand *calli*, each leading to some new vision of beauty; when it seemed we needed no sustenance but the very air – if you would cast your mind back, you might recall one particular evening when, for a few hours, we separated. This in itself would have marked the night as strange, for we were accustomed to spend those long hours in one another's company, sharing that intimate discourse known only to the deepest of friendships. As the sun sank across the *Laguna*, you expressed a wish to experience the city in darkness; I, however, protested some passing nervous exhaustion, some surfeit of stimulation. Your very eagerness sickened me, as if you found in those perambulations some greater purpose that still eluded me, and uncharitable words escaped my lips. You proceeded alone.

Here I must confess, if not a deception, then an omission. I did not stay abed. Within but a few minutes of your departure I bitterly regretted our separation. Setting aside the oppression upon my mind, I hurried out, hoping to find you and take up our mutual pleasure once more.

Perhaps I mistook my way through those shadowy lanes; perhaps I crossed the fourth bridge instead of the third; whatever the cause, I found myself between two towering buildings I did not recognise, their tops almost touching above me. It was terribly dark. I heard, or thought I heard, a mournful cry, like that of a great bird. Turning, I saw before me a stranger. The figure wore an ash-grey cloak and blank white *bauta*, and carried a bright-flamed lantern. I called out, and the shade darted around the corner. I paused, considering whether to flee, to seek the comfort of your company once more. But what could I do but follow?

With each turn, I saw the light ahead, as if waiting for me, and then with billowing cloak the stranger would vanish. How long we passed in this fashion I cannot say, perhaps minutes, perhaps hours, but when I at last thought to look about me and determine my location, we had reached a dark *campiello* that was entirely unfamiliar to me. The visitant stood in the square's centre, beneath a small persimmon tree with buds just beginning to turn to bloom.

As I came close, my quarry lowered that lifeless mask – and I saw this was a woman. I saw dark eyes, an innocent smile, a stray lock of auburn hair. She approached and raised her pale hand to my chest. I experienced the shock of the corporeal as she pressed it there, for I had not imagined that she could be a being of touch, of sense. As a warmth grew beneath her fingers, the light of the lantern grew brighter. I felt her breath upon my face, fresh and sweet. When I opened my mouth to speak, there came a stabbing pain in my heart, as though she had reached inside my very flesh. I cried out, and then – and then…?

I returned to consciousness, leaned against the door of our *pensione*. Checking my watch, still mercifully in its pocket, I saw to my astonishment that less than an hour had passed since your departure. I do not know what occurred in the intervening time, nor how I was able to traverse the maze of night back to our door; nor was I ever able, in the days that followed, despite all my desperate wanderings, to locate the *campiello* with its single persimmon tree. As for that night, with my limbs heavy and my mind clouded, I could only take myself upstairs to bed, my mind turning over the disturbing events until I fell into restless sleep. When I awoke in the morning, you were there once more.

My behaviour in the ensuing days was, I am quite sure, that of a brute. I closed my heart to yours, refusing to disclose even a fragment of my turbulent thoughts. Though you wept and pleaded, I acted as a man unmoved, my very silence a poor mask for the violent strife within my breast. In truth, though I did not know it at first, I was undergoing a second birth, and the pain of it brought separation from the waking world – and from you. While you stepped once more across the bright *Piazza san Marco* and through the exalted halls of the *Gallerie dell'Accademia*, I searched every shadowy corner of the city for a place and a person I could not find. We returned to Edinburgh in near silence.

In the years since, you mentioned our rupture only once, to ask whether I had been beset by some profound doubt or religious terror. The brief, offhand response I gave silenced that subject, and we resumed our correspondence as friends, if now of a different kind. Many nights I have dwelled on what might have been, had it been possible to maintain that intimacy between us, had I not allowed mere distance to work its dreadful magic. Perhaps if I had taken you into my confidence...? But how could I! My life had been consumed by another, in a way beyond words. And so I must turn – my hand, as you may well detect, trembling with the effort of bringing forth what has so long been hidden – to Miss Mackay.

Naturally, I am aware of the rumours regarding my relationship with the prolific poetess, and have granted them only the attention they merit, which is to say none at all. Perhaps you too have wondered if she was the cause of the rift between us – and indeed it is so, though not in the way you imagine. Certainly, it is she who is the cause of my retirement from Edinburgh society to the Sutherland wilderness; certainly, once I had encountered her, once I had fully apprehended the import of her talent for our national literature, I knew that I must commit myself to the nurture of that precious pen. But as to the why, the how, the who? I shall make my best attempt at the explanation you, dear Charles, are so sorely owed.

When I returned to my desk, ensconced in my house on Heriot Row, I undertook a work unlike any I had previously offered the reading public. My little novel, as you know, had brought me some small success, enough at least to fund our travels; my brief volume on the legends of the Gaels had, with your support, been met with no little interest; and yet this new effort marked a great departure. Whereas before I had been guided by workmanlike planning and careful endeavour, now the words spilled forth from my pen as though unbidden. The sorrows of Fearghas and Caitrìona arose from within me, their plight a channel for all I had ever grieved. Yes, I am speaking to you of *The Hill of the Grey Eagle*, and when, after long weeks of incessant effort, pausing only for such brief rest and scraps of bread as were required to maintain the furious labour, the pages were submitted to the publisher by a hand, both mine and not mine, that signed its name – as Miss Malvina Mackay.

I had imagined that, once this work was completed, the madness – for so I thought it at the time – would be gone from me. I had hoped that the novel might suffice as a form of exorcism, to be published in a small edition, read by only a few, and remembered by fewer still. With the dreams sealed away in the book's green covers, I desired only return to my drab and ordinary life. I was not at all prepared for the reception which was to greet my grey eagle, my Malvina. When the first few letters came, I appreciated their interest, though was disturbed by their fervour. When the letters continued to arrive each day in their dozens, I feared the new age that was upon us, and I fled. As I write now, I understand that perhaps I fled not only the weight of the correspondence, but also the very bonds of human society – which is to say, of friendship. Be that as it may, the recent passing of a half-remembered elderly cousin, who left this world, I am sad to say, alone but for the bottle of *uisge-beatha* by his side, made available to me the old manse of Eadar-dà-chaolas. I arrived in winter's dark, through winds blowing direct from the Arctic ice.

Still the letters followed me, forwarded by my assiduous publisher. Her readers, hungering, I fear, for something more true than the moribund sophistication that plagues our presses, saw in Miss Mackay the prophetess of a great Celtic revival. What was I to do?

One evening, when the winds dropped to eerie stillness, I walked out to the darkening shore, not even pausing to don my jacket and boots. I saw three *sgarbhan* fly low and silent over the water. The last light of the sun laid its broken path to *Hy-Brasil*. Behind me, the shadows of mountains cradled the bay. I strode onto a black point that pierced the waves, drawn forward by a force as familiar as it was unnameable, out to the edge of understanding. The surf rolled grey and white around me. I called out, asking the very rocks beneath my feet for guidance, and the cool salt spray splashing across my chest gave me answer. When I returned to the manse, shivering from the cold and more than the cold, I lit a candle and replied to the letters, in her hand and in her name. With each stroke of the pen, her mind grew stronger.

In the two decades since *The Hill*, Miss Mackay has published eight novels, three volumes of verse, and two compendia of folklore. Each was written in the same spiritual frenzy as that first tale of the grey eagle. Each found a wider readership than the last; each furthered Miss Mackay's reputation as the foremost chronicler of the nation of *Alba;* and yet she has never appeared in person to respond to such acclaim. Each query has been given the same answer.

> Miss Mackay prefers to remain in her ancestral lands, between the two straits, where the broad Atlantic beats on Sutherland's rocky shores, where the pure rivers nourish her creative vitality, where the *sùlairean* drop like spears into the sea.

This is nothing less than the truth. When I leave the manse to take the air of sea and mountain, when I return to the heat and smoke of my good peat fire, I know for certain that Miss Mackay is no imposture or deceit, but in truth a second consciousness brought forth within my own body. She is all that is good within me, a renewed expression of that great spirit which surpasses our brief, individual lives.

What occurred in Venice, there in the heart of Europe, was a bolt from the heavens, awakening the first stirrings of that spirit. The ensuing mental turmoil occasioned my cruel treatment of you who was closest to me, who was most in danger of perceiving the split through my centre. My most profound regret is that I have not yet granted you the honest intimacy with Miss Mackay that you deserved. Let me now be clear: though you have corresponded with her often in the intervening years – on the role of the Gaelic language in our cultural revival, on the indifference of the City to such work, straying even as far as the dangerous waters of the Irish question – you have never understood Miss Malvina Mackay as a soul who resides within the mortal husk of that melancholy man, James Straiton, alongside, which is to say, within and without, his own. This, then, was the lie: not that Malvina never existed, but that she is, and has always been, your friend. For this, I am most truly sorry.

Those few who share the knowledge of Miss Mackay's nature are sworn to secrecy. I cannot blame our colleague, Mr Drummond, for his assumption that you were one of the number, and thus for the comments that so perplexed you and which prompted your letter. I pray that this reply restores some of the faith you once had in us both. If there are questions still to answer, I would extend you an invitation: to travel from London to Edinburgh, from there north to Inverness, and then on to Sutherland and our home, *Taigh an Lochain*. The road is long and uneven, but the view of the great northern mountains reflected on the waters will more than suffice as recompense. You will find the accommodations modest but comfortable, and you will meet there both an old friend and a new one. Miss Mackay would be glad to answer all that you put to her, as would I,

Yours in regret and hope,

James Straiton
on behalf of Mal-mhìne NicAoidh

On Being Brought from Africa to America

Fred D'Aguiar

'Twas mercy brought me from my Pagan land,
Taught my benighted soul to understand
That there's a God, that there's a Saviour too:
Once I redemption neither sought nor knew.
Some view our sable race with scornful eye,
"Their colour is a diabolic die."
Remember, Christians, Negros, black as Cain,
May be refin'd, and join th' angelic train.

> 'On Being Brought from Africa to America'
> by Phillis Wheatley

His darling child asked him if she could go outside to play with the other girls and boys and he said no. He said no without knowing why. He spoke out of turn with a hunch that saying no to his daughter was what he should say. She begged him right away. She did not wait, skip a beat before she launched her long, please Dad, please, please, please. Her father shook his head and closed his eyes to shut her out. His daughter's little body twisted as she begged him. Her lids started to flood with her father's refusal as she kept on with her plea to him.

He told her to ask her mother. That her mother will be back from the market soon. He reminded his daughter that her mother prefers it if she stays in the house when one or other parent is not at home. That was the last thing her mother said to me and to our daughter. She was standing right here next to me when her mother said it.

Nevertheless she persisted with her request. She begged her father over and over. As she kept on it began to sound more like a demand than a request.

She said that all of her friends were playing just outside in the yard. That her father could hear her play and see her as well if he craned his neck out of the window. She promised she would not go far. She promised him. The way she said please to him, dragging it out, it sounded as if it took twelve letters to spell the word.

Well, he could not concentrate. He stopped his wood-carving and lifted his eyes from the small wood figure in front of him and gazed at his daughter as she begged him. Her eyes brimmed with tears and she twisted and turned from left to right, which picked up pace and became frantic. He did not want her to fall over in front of him and for her eyes to spill out of her head. Not on account of him saying no to her simple request. He relented.

He told her to stay within earshot. He said if she saw her mother coming up the road she should run back inside the house.

His daughter thanked him over and over as she slipped out of the house. Her last words to him were, Dad. You are the best.

Of course he knew that he was the best, only for now, until he had to tell her no on another occasion and stick to it. He would have been the best in everyone's eyes – though temporarily not in hers – if he had only ignored her begging him, put up with her falling over and crying the front of her dress wet, and kept her safe inside.

Her mother arrived from the market with a few things balanced on her head and her arms free to fan the unmoving air for some cool. She opened the door to be met by quiet and stillness. Not the quiet and stillness of her husband's mindful industry, and her daughter caught up with small chores conducted at close quarters. Nor the still and quiet as they waited for her return before their bluster around her. Just this empty place. Her husband and daughter absent from it. She called for her daughter. She called for her husband. She dropped her basket and ran out of the house in the opposite direction to the market.

She ran and called for them. Her eyes flew everywhere. All she wanted her eyes to land on was her daughter and her husband. She had left her daughter washed and dressed and with a few chores to get her through the morning. She had left her daughter with her father who was busy with his carving. She had asked him to keep their daughter close to him and he had said yes, just as she had always asked. He had always obliged, not because she had asked him to do it but for both of them. He knew he had to keep their daughter close by. She was a child. Keep her near him until she grew big and was able to look after herself.

She pictured her daughter. Though strong she was small for her seven years. A pillow cover made a whole dress for her. Two plaits ordered all the hair on her head. A few wipes cleaned her from head to toe. She could sweep up her daughter with one hand, cradle her in the crook of her arm and still balance a basket on her head. Her daughter was a slip of a thing.

The child's father returned to the house alone. Empty-handed. His look said everything. Eyes wide, mouth open, his forehead creased. Since returned, his wife said to him,

You are not coming back to me without our daughter.

He fell to his knees and grabbed the earth and said over and over that he was sorry. His wife had more questions than words to ask him. She just kept saying for want of saying something,

Where is our daughter? Where is she? Where?

She looked around as if her child might jump out of a corner and sparkle in front of her and banish her worry. Her husband crumpled at her feet. He looked as if he stooped in the middle of his prayers.

He had heard his daughter. She played so close by it was as if she were standing before him. She played just outside the window. She sang and clapped her hands with two of her friends. He carved and fitted things together with a few knocks of his hammer and listened and heard his daughter. He did this carving and hammering and listening for his daughter for some time. At some point he stopped, not to listen for his daughter but just not to separate one thing from the other, as if his woodwork and her play were one and the same varied sound.

It was midday. Time for them to pray. His ears said to him, Where are you child? She was no longer present, no longer there in the middle of his work-noise with her song and clap of hands. He stopped his chisel, gripped it tighter. He leaned his head towards the window. And the quiet took on a hard feel to it, made him drop his chisel and run outside. The last thing the mother said to her daughter, before she left on a few errands was, stay in the house with your father, and make sure you say your midday prayers, and none of your tricks young lady. Her daughter was always busy with something when it was time to help her mother and her father.

She would say, Mum I'll pick up all of my belongings as soon as I finish this one thing that I am doing for father and you.

What thing? her mother would ask, falling for the bait. What can you be doing for your father and me that is more important than gathering all of these bits and pieces spread everywhere and tripping me up?

And the child would say,

I am making a picture of Dad and you and me fetching water from the river.

At this point her mother would forget the long list of chores meant for her daughter and take those chores as things that a mother could do just as easily since her daughter was busy.

What a trick! Her mother smiled at how her child ran rings around her. The mother did not feel tricked at all. She felt blessed. To have a daughter so young and with such a wise head on her shoulders. Whatever the child was making for her parents had to be better than some chore or other.

The child's father prayed that his daughter could hear him. He knew she could, *inshallah*, hear his prayers. He wanted her to know that she was loved by him and by her mother. That, as her father, he had forgotten her only for that moment he worked. In that fleeting drop of his guard of her, slavers had captured her. In his prayers he begs Allah for forgiveness for his failure to protect his child. His wife tells him that he did not fail their daughter, that trying to save her would only have meant throwing his life away. That, had he done so, his wife would be without her daughter and without her husband too. That Allah made him *not* think about their daughter for an instant to keep him safe with his wife, rather than have her lose both her child and her husband. That she would be dead by her own hand for sure, a mortal sin, had her husband not been there to greet her when she returned to the half-empty village.

As a mother her head and heart hurt for her daughter. She felt the same hurt in her stomach and in her sleep all day and every day with her daughter gone. Both parents felt this hurt. Her father hurt even more having been the one who was responsible for the care of their daughter. They prayed loud and long that Allah in his mercy may grant her safe passage wherever she may be and that, being merciful, Allah may grant her safe return to them.

Her mother spreads her daughter's things around the house just to fall over them. Just to pick up those things piece by piece, made glad again that her daughter tricked her into tidying up. Maybe her daughter was still playing a trick on her parents. To make them think that she was gone and have them come close to believing that their daughter might never return, only for her to pop up, large as life, and say, Mother, Father, you found me, it is me, your daughter!

The child prayed to Allah, in whose mercy she believed that she lived, and who decreed that this ship take her from her mother and father. To keep her in the middle of this big sea. Under the swell of this water. Below fish. Prayed for a heaven after this life underwater.

She saw water without end, the dip and sway of the vessel that swallowed her, and hundreds like her.

Hands slapped her. Tongues lashed out at her. Hands threw water over her to keep her awake, to make her clean. Her captors presented themselves as her saviours.

People examined her from head to toe, checked her whole body, her teeth, her hair, between her toes and between her legs. They gave her their name. They gave her the name of the ship that placed a roof on the sea and carried her in its belly.

She saw clouds that reminded her of her village, the fields and trees around her home.

She thought that she sailed in the belly of a whale. There were hundreds like her. They threw some of the sick and the rebellious into the sea. Some of them jumped into the sea for salvation. Jumped for the land under the sea, far from this ship, far from these people who chained them and beat them.

The child's ears filled with cries and shouting and whiplashes. Soon she ceased hearing. She replaced those cries with the call to prayer. She practised in her mind's eye the movements of praying alongside her mother within earshot and sight of her father.

Alhamdu Lillahi Rabbil Aalamin.

The days she lost count of – time now punctuated by whip and spit, vomit and dying. The ship cut into the sea as if sinking deeper and deeper down amidst the salt and air and cloud and sky, no birds, no trees, no land.

The child started to forget. She was made to forget her name. She clamped her teeth and lips to avoid saying something that might draw lashes. Soon the child's tongue buried itself for safety deep into her body. Her name, so long kept a secret, she no longer knew. She no longer possessed a mother and father to call it, or have her answer to it and run to meet them.

She lay below deck and walked above with other children. She was not a child or a girl. She emptied everything that belonged to her into the sea.

She was no longer allowed to pray her way. She was surrounded by the dying and the sea that parted for those thrown or jumping into it, always the same open arms of the sea. All around her and the other children.

Her tongue died in her mouth. Another tongue replaced it, something new, with traces of the old. Something that started to fill the hollowed out and empty shell of the child. Torn from her flesh and blood. Lifted off the land where she grew, that her navel string was buried in, and swallowed by a whale, swallowed in turn by the sea, by history.

The sea, and everything beyond it, made her forget the land that she left and her mother and father and her saviour. The sea made a promise to her. Saltwater said to her, *Forget your former life. Forget what you left behind you before you were captured. Empty yourself that you may be filled anew.* The child tried her best to think and keep thinking that there was a place beyond this sea where her father and mother were waiting for her to jump from her hiding place and say, Mother, Father, it is me!

Contributors

David Almond OBE is the author of *Skellig, The Tightrope Walkers, The Dam, Island* and many more novels, stories, picture books, plays and opera librettos. His work has been translated into 40 languages and has won many major awards, including The Carnegie Medal, The Nonino International Prize, and The Hans Christian Andersen Award, the world's most prestigious prize for children's authors. He lives on the North East coast.

Leila Aboulela is the first-ever winner of the Caine Prize for African Writing. She is the author of six novels *River Spirit, Bird Summons, The Kindness of Enemies, Minaret, The Translator* and *Lyrics Alley*, Fiction Winner of the Scottish Book Awards. Her short story collection *Elsewhere, Home*, won the Saltire Fiction Book of the Year. Leila's work has been translated into fifteen languages and she was long-listed three times for the Orange Prize (now the Women's Prize for Fiction). Leila grew up in Sudan and now lives in Scotland.

Fred D'Aguiar's books include poetry, fiction, plays and a memoir. His most recent publications are a memoir,

Year of Plagues, a collection of poetry, *Letters to America,* and a pamphlet, *Grace Notes.* Born in London in 1960 of Guyanese parents, he grew up in Guyana and returned to the UK for his secondary and tertiary education. He is currently Professor of English at UCLA.

Jenni Fagan was born in Scotland. Jenni was selected as one of Granta's Best Young British Novelists after the publication of her debut novel, *The Panopticon,* which was shortlisted for the Desmond Elliott Prize and the James Tait Black Prize. Her following novels, *The Sunlight Pilgrims* and *Luckenbooth* have been shortlisted for numerous awards. She has won the Scottish Author of the Year at the Herald Culture Award and is a Doctor of Philosophy.

Cathy Forde is a Scottish writer whose novels include *Fat Boy Swim, Skarrs* and *The Drowning Pond.* Her drama includes *Empty* for National Theatre of Scotland, *Helping Hands* for Pitlochry Festival Theatre and *Baby's Coming Home* for BBC Radio. She is currently adapting *Fat Boy Swim* into a musical with Visible Fictions.

Harry Josephine Giles is a writer and performer from Orkney, living in Leith. Their verse novel *Deep Wheel Orcadia* was published by Picador in October 2021 and won the Arthur C. Clarke Award for Science Fiction Book of the Year.

Pippa Goldschmidt has a background in astronomy and is the author of a novel, *The Falling Sky,* and a collection of short stories, *The Need for Better Regulation of Outer Space*, and most recently co-edited *Uncanny Bodies*. Her work has been broadcast on BBC Radio 4 and recently published in Gutter, ArtReview, Tamarind, Times Literary Supplement and Magma.

Jessie Greengrass is the author of two novels: *Sight*, which was shortlisted for the 2018 Women's Prize for Fiction and *The High House*, shortlisted for the Costa Novel Prize 2021. Her collection of short stories, *An Account of the Decline of the Great Auk, According to One Who Saw It* won the Edge Hill Prize 2016.

Hannah Lavery is a Scottish poet and playwright. She was appointed Edinburgh Makar (or City Poet) in November 2021 for a three year term and has been selected for the Scottish Best Poem twice. Her plays include *The Drift*, *Lament for Sheku Bayoh* and *Protest!* She is an associate artist with the National Theatre of Scotland and one of the winners of the Peggy Ramsay/Film4 Award 2022.

PK Lynch is an actor and writer. She is the author of two novels – *Armadillos* (Sceptre Prize for Fiction; Not the Booker longlist; Amazon Rising Star nominee) and *Wildest of All*. Her first play, *Promise*, was longlisted for the Bruntwood Prize and *King of the Gypsies* was an Edinburgh Fringe Recommended Show by The Scotsman which toured nationally.

Kirsty Williams is a producer and director at BBC Scotland, where she's made audio drama and readings for BBC Radio 4 and BBC Sounds for the past 20 years. As a story editor she supports factual teams to deliver narrative podcasts to international audiences.